D0292785

"You know what ... Jacob's voice let ... "toys" he was referring to.

Em took a big gulp. "I think so."

He stared at her, the kind of deep, dark, edgy look that might have sent her running if it hadn't been him. But she knew him now, and his bark was far worse than his bite.

At least, she hoped so.

"There are toys for every kind of sex adventure the hotel guests could want."

She took another gulp. "I know. I want...I want to see."

He muttered something to himself that sounded like "Don't do it, Hill," rubbing the day-old growth on his jaw in agitation.

She wanted to feel the roughness of it against her skin. "Show me," she whispered.

"I must be insane. Insane." He walked away a few feet, then stalked back, taking her hand. "Come on, then."

She wanted to tell him not to worry, it would be okay. But of course it wouldn't. Nothing would ever be okay again.

Blaze™

Dear Reader,

It's been a while since I wrote a book for Harlequin Blaze.
Too long. In fact, I'd wondered if I would remember
how.... But happily it was like getting on a bike. Fun,
exhilarating and always exciting.

This story is part of the DO NOT DISTURB series,
which takes place in the plush, exotic hotel Hush in
New York City. The setting itself was a character, as
the hotel caters to the...um, let's call it the sensually
adventurous. I singed my fingertips writing a couple of
the scenes.... I wonder if you'll be able to tell which ones.

I hope you've enjoyed reading DO NOT DISTURB. And
don't forget to check out eHarlequin.com for related
online stories.

In the meantime, check in to Hush...and enjoy the fun.

Jill Shalvis

Books by Jill Shalvis
HARLEQUIN BLAZE
  63—NAUGHTY BUT NICE
 132—BARED

HARLEQUIN TEMPTATION
  938—LUKE
 962—BACK IN THE BEDROOM
 995—SEDUCE ME
1015—FREE FALL

ROOM SERVICE

Jill Shalvis

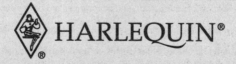

TORONTO • NEW YORK • LONDON
AMSTERDAM • PARIS • SYDNEY • HAMBURG
STOCKHOLM • ATHENS • TOKYO • MILAN • MADRID
PRAGUE • WARSAW • BUDAPEST • AUCKLAND

ISBN 0-373-79236-0

ROOM SERVICE

Copyright © 2006 by Jill Shalvis.

This edition published by arrangement with Harlequin Books S.A.

® and TM are trademarks of the publisher. Trademarks indicated with
® are registered in the United States Patent and Trademark Office, the
Canadian Trade Marks Office and in other countries.

www.eHarlequin.com

Printed in U.S.A.

Prologue

Los Angeles

EMMA HARRIS WAS PART Hollywood business shark, part Ohio farm girl, and though that might seem like an odd combination, it had always worked for her.

Until now.

Now she was a twenty-seven-year-old TV producer facing her last chance in this business. If she blew it, then goodbye job, goodbye career, goodbye to it all because she'd be washed up. Done, finished, finito, before she'd even hit the big three-oh.

But she was too determined, too stubborn, to allow that to happen. Of course, it didn't help that everyone at the production company she worked for thought her luck had run out, including her own assistant, who'd quit last week to go to work as a grip at an NBC sitcom. But Em would never give up.

Nope, she was made of sterner stuff than that. She'd grown up in Ohio, on a thriving family farm, which she'd left to go to college and then produce television shows. Her parents were still horrified, certain that a girl like her, with strong morals and ethics, couldn't possibly make a go of it in Hollywood, but she was dead set on proving them wrong.

She *loved* this job. She simply wouldn't believe she couldn't make it work, her way.

But she'd been summoned by the boss…reminding her that determination was not enough, not in Hollywood. Drawing a deep breath, she made the long walk from her office to his. Outside his closed door, she smoothed her skirt, decided there was no hope for her hair so she didn't even try and, after pasting a smile over her worried frown, knocked with every ounce of confidence and authority she had.

"Come in!"

Em opened the door. From the big leather chair behind his big, fancy network desk, Nathan Bennett scowled.

Em locked her smile in place. "You wanted to see me?"

"Emmaline Harris. Sit."

Great, her full name. Never a good sign. She entered and sat where he indicated—a smaller, far less comfortable-looking chair, which was there, she knew, to make people feel inferior.

She wouldn't let it work. After all, she'd been raised with her mother's words ringing in her ears. "Em," she'd say, hands on her hips, her jeans dirty from hard work. "No one can make you feel inferior without your consent."

A quote from Eleanor Roosevelt, of course, and Em had always believed it. She *was* tough enough for this town!

Nathan looked at her for a long moment, as if measuring his words carefully. "Do you know why you're here today?"

To be fired. Unless she could fast-talk her way back. Which she could do, she told herself. She could fast-talk with the best of them. It was lying and manipulation she had trouble with. "I'm pretty certain."

Nathan nodded, looking stern and unhappy, and Em felt as if she was sitting in front of the principal, only this was worse, far worse, because being ousted here meant so much more than a few days suspension without homework. It meant bye-bye paycheck.

But she would not be saying bye-bye to her self-respect. Nope, if she was going down, then she'd go down with pride intact.

Nathan steepled his fingers. "We hired you, Emmaline, in spite of your utter lack of experience in this business, because we thought you were a bright star on the horizon, just waiting to make her mark."

"Sir—"

"We thought you'd do great things for our production company."

"And I hope I'm just getting started." She tried the smile again.

It still wasn't returned.

Instead, Nathan rearranged his already perfectly arranged pencil and pen set to the right of his spotless blotter. "Emmaline, can you explain the last three shows you produced here?"

"Well, I—"

"And why each failed?"

Her smile faltered. Yes, she could. But she wouldn't. Because that would mean hurting others. When she'd first come to town, she hadn't understood the rules—or, rather, that there were no rules. She got it now, the challenge being to make that work to her benefit without compromising herself. "I'm sure everyone here has had some trouble at one time or another," she said. "Three failures in the whole, big scheme of things—"

"These were your *only* shows, Em. You're batting zero here."

They both knew she was a hard worker, that wasn't the problem. In fact, she'd been throwing herself headlong into every project from her first set of LEGO at age three, and had been told time and time again by her family and teachers that she was made of pure tenacity and grit.

Unfortunately she had a soft heart to go with that drive, which often threw a wrench into being the best of the best. Because she wouldn't lie, nor would she hurt anyone or anything on her way to the top. She couldn't live with herself if she did.

Which was why she couldn't explain to Nathan about the failures of her three shows. "I know my record looks bad, but I can do this, Nathan. Please, just give me another shot. If I could just have the reins of a show from the very beginning—"

Already shaking his head, he leaned back in his chair. His hair was black, devoid of any gray, and with a similar comb-over style to Donald Trump's. His face was tanned from his last vacation in the Bahamas with the third wife, and he wore diamond studs in his ears that could pay Em's salary for at least five years. He'd probably never been fired in his life. "You've had your shot," he said firmly. "*Three* of them."

Sure. First up had been the exciting reality show involving two brothers, both sweet and adorable inventors, with IQs off the map. Em had thought Ty and Todd so wonderful, and because they'd been struggling to make ends meet, too, she'd made it her personal mission to get the word out on them. Only as it turned out, Ty and Todd had failed to mention the word had been out once before, and that they were in court for patent infringements. By the time the first episode aired, both the network and Nathan had been sued.

With failure ringing in her ears, Em's second attempt had been her chance to prove the previous disaster had been an unlucky break. But right from the beginning, the crew on the safari-adventure-themed reality show had fought viciously amongst themselves, backstabbing and sabotaging at will. Because Em hadn't been allowed to hire them in the first place, she'd been left in the position of being unable to control them. That, coupled with the fact that not one of them could read a map, and it had been a "lost" cause before they'd even begun.

Em's third and last effort had been a talk show where, not-so-coincidentally, the host had been Nathan's niece by marriage. A lovely, funny, sharp woman making her way up the ranks in the comic circuit, a woman who'd had an incredibly unlucky streak in life culminating in a horrific car accident the year before and was now, secretly and unfortunately, addicted to her prescription meds. A secret, of course, that could ruin her. When Em had discovered it, the woman had begged and cried and pleaded for Em not to tell.

Of course Em didn't tell, it wasn't in her genetic makeup to do such a thing, but when the comic had self-destructed—on live TV—the decision had cost Em the show, garnering her the knowledge that she didn't want to work with relatives of her boss ever again.

Now she had three failures like balls on a chain around her neck. Each had occurred, Em was certain, not because she was a bad producer, but because she'd been handed the cast and crew instead of picking them herself.

The stakes had never been higher, she knew this. But she also knew anything was possible, including making it in this business. Her way. "I can do this, Nathan," she said again. "I know I can. You just have to give me a real chance to do so."

"Emmaline—"

"A *real* chance." She stood, putting her hands on his desk, leaning in, desperate to make him see how badly she wanted this. "If I could pick the crew and the host this time—"

"You don't have any experience in that area."

True enough. Until college, she'd driven a tractor, she'd run a hay barn and she'd managed the books for the dairy division of her family's farm.

Having graduated from college with a business degree in TV development, she knew it was time to hold down a job in her field, not a hay field. And she wanted it to be *this* job. "You saw something in me, you just said it. Please, let me try again, just one more time."

Nathan twirled a mechanical pencil in his fingers and did that long silent pause that always made Em want to squirm. Finally he let out a long sigh. "I know I'm going to be sorry, but…yeah."

"Yeah?" In shock, she laughed. *"Really?"*

Looking unhappy about it, he nodded.

"Oh, my God, thank you thank you thank you," she cried, running around his desk to throw her arms around him.

Awkwardly, he patted her on the back. "Okay now."

"I'm sorry." She dropped her arms and stepped back, but she still couldn't swipe the wide grin off her face. "You won't regret this, not for a minute."

"Just promise me you're really going to make this work," he said solemnly to her face-splitting smile, though if she wasn't mistaken, his eyes did actually twinkle. "Because, trust me, Em, if you screw this up, you're done in this business for good."

"Oh, I'm going to make this work." She inhaled deeply to keep from hugging him again. "So tell me… what kind of show is it going to be?"

She envisioned another talk show, or maybe a well-written, sharp, witty sitcom. Yeah, that would be so perfect, something that would make people laugh—

"We want a cooking thing."

Em stared at him, some of her elation fading. "A cooking thing."

"With a dynamic chef who can really entertain. You

know, juggle knives, toss the ingredients around. Like those chefs at the Japanese restaurants, only without the ethnicity. You'll cook everything across the board on this show, from burgers to beef tartare."

Tartare? She didn't even know what that was. "A cooking show," she repeated, thoughts racing. Unfortunately, she didn't know the inner workings of a kitchen any more than she understood the aerodynamics of a plane.

"Cooking shows are hot right now," Nathan said.

A cooking show, when Em could burn water without trying.

"You should start with the chef. He'll be the key to your success. I actually have one in mind—"

"But you just said I could hire—"

"The staff to *support* the show."

She fixed her smile back in place, adding an easy nod that she hoped covered up the panic hurtling through her veins instead of blood. *Cooking* show… "I was hoping you'd trust me to hire everyone for the show."

"I do. Just go check out the chef I have in mind. He has charisma in spades. He'd draw the audience right in. Women think he's sexy as hell, too."

"Who is he?"

"Chef Jacob Hill, currently running Amuse Bouche, the world-class restaurant inside Hush, an equally world-class hotel in New York."

"You mean that new hotel that's themed for…"

"Sex? Yep, that's the one. You can leave ASAP." Nathan stopped and looked at her. "Oh, one more thing."

She was still reeling from the fact that she wasn't

fired, that she was doing a cooking show and that she was headed to a hotel that specialized in sexual exploration and adventure.

"I know your potential, Em. It's why I'm doing this. But listen to me. You're going to have to…"

"What?"

He sighed. "Harden that ridiculously soft heart of yours. Toughen up."

"I'm plenty tough."

"Not in the way I'm talking. It'd help if you learned to conform to the way we do things around here."

"You mean like lie and cheat?"

He offered her a smile, his first. "Exactly. If that chef won't come willingly? Hire someone to find a hair on their plate at Amuse Bouche. In a place like that, he'd be ruined instantly. He'll be begging to do the show."

She stared at him. "That's despicable."

He shrugged. "That's life."

"I would never do something like that."

"Yeah." His smile faded and he scrubbed his hands over his face. "Here comes number four."

"I am *not* failing a fourth time."

He didn't look convinced, but to his credit, he didn't say so. "You've got yourself one month to get this show off the ground. Go break a leg."

She moved to the door when he opened it for her, feeling a little stunned, a little overwhelmed, a little excited and a lot sick.

"Good luck," Nathan said wryly.

No doubt, she was going to need it.

1

New York

THREE DAYS LATER EM stood in the gorgeous lobby of Hotel Hush, looking around in marvel. The carpet beneath her feet was a pattern of blacks, greens, grays and pinks, and felt so thick it was like walking on air. The grand furniture and artwork on the vast walls brought to mind the great old salons of the roaring twenties.

She knew from Hush's Web site that the place catered to the young, wealthy and daring. It was eighty guest rooms of fun, flirty sophistication and excitement, with additional offerings such as designer penthouse suites complete with personal butlers, an "it" bar named Erotique that attracted the glitterati of New York, a luxurious spa, a rooftop swimming pool...

And every available amenity was geared toward Hush's hook: erotic fun. Guests could use their room's private video camera complete with blank tapes, or any of the "toys" in each armoire. And downstairs in the basement was a discreet entertainment parlor where couples could engage in semiprivate exhibition fantasies, and more.

"More" being sensual pleasures that only those with an extremely open, worldly point of view would dare experience. According to the info Em had gotten online, anything could be obtained here, tried here, seen here. Anything at all.

Em couldn't even imagine the half of it. Not that it mattered. She wasn't here for the pleasures. She was here to see Amuse Bouche, and its chef. Nathan had chosen well. It was rumored that Chef Jacob Hill was unparalleled in the kitchen, any kitchen, and that he was a virtual modern-day god.

And wildly, fabulously sexy to boot.

People said that his food was out of this world, that once you ate something he cooked, you fell for him hook, line and sinker. They said that his waitstaff had to guard the doors to the kitchen, beating women off with a stick every night.

She hoped that translated to great TV.

She'd tried to learn more about him, but interestingly enough there wasn't much to learn. She'd found several lists of impressive credentials, but with an odd omission— anything prior to five years ago was a complete blank.

Which meant either Chef Jacob Hill was relatively new to his field, or he had a past he didn't care to advertise.

An enigma.

And the last piece to the puzzle of Em's success.

Hopefully he had one element common with the rest of the human race, that he could be coaxed, by either the promise of money or fame, all the way across the country to L.A.

"Look at this place," Liza said in awe. Liza was Em's oldest friend and newest assistant. That she looked like Barbara Eden circa *I Dream of Jeannie* had turned out to be invaluable in the industry as far as getting things done her way. Which was good, as Liza, never a warm, fuzzy sort, never one to back off from a good fight, liked to get her way. This made her an extremely efficient assistant, if a rather fierce one.

"They sure take the art deco theme seriously, don't they?" She looked all around them. "This stuff is all museum quality."

"Yeah, I'm sure that's why the male guests come here." This from Eric, Em's second-closest friend, and new location director. He was looking at a bold, bright painting of a very beautiful and very nude woman stretched out on a luxurious daybed for all to see—and he was enjoying the view greatly, if the smile on his face was anything to judge by. "The *quality.*"

Liza rolled her eyes. "We're here for the restaurant."

"Yeah, and trust me, as a chef, good restaurants hold a special place in my heart, but we're really here to save Em's ass— *Oomph.*" Rubbing the ribs Liza had just elbowed, he glared at her. "What? It's true."

Liza shook her head in disgust. "It's not true, and you're not a chef."

"Am so."

"Are not."

Em sighed. The two of them possessed a unique talent for getting a reaction out of each other, be it annoyance—or sexual tension.

Eric went back to ogling the nudes.

"You're a dog," Liza said to him. "Men are dogs."

"Woof, woof," Eric said.

If Eric was a dog, he was a good-looking one—tall and very Californian in his casual chinos, untucked polo shirt, tennis shoes and sunglasses shoved to the top of his blond mop. He had eyes the color of an azure sky, and could stop traffic with a single smile.

Also handy when it came to getting his way.

Em couldn't do this without either of them.

"I'm going to check in," Liza said. "I'm getting a room as far from yours—" she pointed at Eric "—as possible."

"Works for me." Eric gave a careless shrug. "Last chance, Em. Save yourself all the trouble and use me as your chef. You know I'm good."

He *was* good, but not formally trained, and such a goofball that no one ever took him seriously. She was afraid that would be apparent on the TV screen. "Eric—" Emma said.

"Yeah, yeah. I'm going to the bar."

"Works for me," Liza snapped, and with a mutual growl, both of them were gone, leaving Em standing in the lobby alone. "Well," she said to herself. "This is going to be fun."

The three of them together had always been fun before. They'd made their way through college, existing on fun.

That is, until last year. That had been when Eric had been stupid enough to tell Liza he loved her, then given her a diamond ring and married her.

The marriage—based on fun and lust—had lasted for

two wild, sexually charged months before they'd had an explosive fight. And because neither of them had ever had a real relationship, neither of them had known what to do with real love. Now, with all that emotion still pent up inside them, with no way to deal with it, they snarled and growled and bickered.

Em loved both of them, but if they didn't realize that they just needed to trust themselves—and get back in the sack—then she was going to lock them together in the same room until they figured it out for themselves.

Another time, though. Because right now, Eric was right. She had to save herself. To that end, she walked toward check-in. The front desk had the same sexy sophistication as the rest of the lobby, with its chest-high black marble counters. The wall behind matched, broken only by the neon-pink *HUSH* blazing in the center.

The check-in process was handled by a pretty woman wearing a black tux with a pink tie and a friendly smile. "Twelfth floor, same as your friends. Room 1212 for you. It's got a great view of the city and should have everything you need. Feel free to call us for anything."

If only it were that easy. Just call the front desk for Chef Jacob Hill... She took the room key with a wry smile and caught up with Liza and Eric at the elevators.

Eric held out a beer, lifting it in a toast. "This place is really something. You can actually smell the excitement in the air."

Liza inhaled and shrugged.

Eric laughed. "This place is for people who want a rush, who want to feel cosmopolitan, exotic. *I* feel it."

"Since when did you ever want cosmopolitan, Mr. Beer-on-the-couch-with-the-remote?" Liza asked.

"Since two women in Erotique practically lapped me up just now."

Liza's eyes fired with temper but she merely inquired, "Erotique?"

"The bar. You should have seen me in there. Hot stuff, baby." He waggled his eyebrows. "You should have kept me while you had the chance."

"Ha."

Appearing happy to have irritated the thorn in his side, Eric smiled at Em. "Here's to phase two," he said and lifted his beer in another toast. "To getting our TV chef."

Liza nodded. "To Em's success."

"Absolutely." Eric's eyes locked on hers and went warm, his smile genuine.

Liza's slowly faded.

"What?" he asked. "What's the matter?"

Liza shook her head. "Did we just…*agree* on something?"

He laughed. "Doubt it."

"No, we did."

"Mark the calendar," he said softly. "Hell must have frozen over."

"You're a funny guy."

"No, it's true." He stepped closer to her. "When we were married, you'd disagree with me no matter what I said. I'd say, 'honey, the sky is blue,' and you'd say, 'nope, it's light blue. Maybe dark blue. But not just blue, because I wouldn't want to agree with you on anything, even a frigging color thing.'"

Liza took a step toward him this time, her body leaning forward. "That's *not* what I did."

Their noses nearly touched. "Truth hurts, doesn't it, babe?"

The two of them were breathing heavily, tension dripping off them in waves, and not all of it anger.

"Guys," Em said.

"You know what's the matter with you?" Liza asked Eric.

"No, but I'm guessing you're about to tell me."

"*Guys?*" Em said again.

"You think you're God's gift to women," Liza said to Eric. "It's obnoxious."

"I'll try to keep it to myself then," Eric said lightly. "Thanks."

"This was stupid," Liza said. "Being here, the two of us."

"Right. Em, you want to give up on this whole chef search and just use me? Seeing as I'm God's gift and all? Then we can all go home."

"We're doing this," Em said. "You guys can do this. Please."

Eric looked at Liza. Liza looked back. Both sighed and nodded.

Em let out a breath. She'd done her research. She was as prepared as it got. They needed Jacob Hill, and she intended to get him.

Her way.

As they waited for the elevator doors to open, Liza scoped out a gorgeous man walking through the lobby.

Eric watched her, eyes shuttered.

Em sighed, then bent to pet a sleek black cat who'd showed up out of nowhere, wearing a bright pink collar with a tag that read Eartha Kitty. With a purr, Eartha Kitty wound around Em's ankles until the elevator doors finally opened.

Em stepped on. The inside was as plush as the rest of the place, lined with mirrors and decorative black steel. As she contemplated the row of glowing pink buttons, the doors began to close—without Liza and Eric, who were facing each other and once again bickering over something or another.

Fed up, determined to do this with or without them, Em pushed the twelfth-floor button. The doors slid all the way closed, and blessed silence reigned. With a sigh, she leaned back against the mirror, closing her eyes. If Liza and Eric didn't kill each other by sunset, she'd happily do the deed herself.

No, better yet, she'd lock them up in one of the rooms here and let them work out their frustrations.

Unfortunately, Em had no outlet for *her* frustrations. Most of the men in her life had turned out to be toads. Okay, *all* of them had turned out to be toads, and though she'd kissed quite a few while looking for her prince, he hadn't yet showed up.

Opening her eyes, she caught a glance of herself. Yikes. Hair wild, eyes tired…if a prince showed up today, he'd go running at the sight of her. She closed her eyes again, opening them only when the doors slid back, revealing…the second level?

How had that happened?

A man stepped into the elevator. He wore black Levi's and battered boots, and a black long-sleeved shirt with the pink *HUSH* logo on his pec. His eyes were covered with mirrored aviator sunglasses, and when he shoved them to the top of his head and looked at Em, her heart stopped. Not because he was drop-dead gorgeous. No, that description felt too neat, too pat, too…*GQ*. In fact, he was the furthest thing from *GQ* she'd ever seen.

He was tall, probably six-four, all tough and rangy and hard-muscled. His hair was cropped extremely short, and was as dark as his fathomless eyes, which were set in a face that could encourage the iciest of women to ache. And that face told the tale that he'd lived every single one of his years as fast and hard as he could.

Which wasn't to say he wasn't appealing. In truth, she couldn't tear her eyes off him. But she could tell he was the kind of man who would worry his mother, the kind of man who would worry a father with a daughter. He seemed…streetwise, tough as nails, edgy, possibly even dangerous.

And then he smiled.

Yeah, big and rough, and most definitely badass. This was a man who'd seen and done things, the sort of man who could walk through a brawl, give as good as he got, and come out unscathed.

A warrior.

Em would have sworn her heart gave one last little flutter before it stopped altogether.

But the most surprising thing was what he said.

"Good, you're here."

Um…what? *Her?* Em looked behind her, but they were alone. *Me?* she mouthed, pointing to herself, nearly swallowing her tongue when he nodded.

"You." His voice wasn't hard and cold, as she might have expected, but quiet and deep, and tinged with a hint of the South, which only added to the ache in her belly.

What was it about a man with a hint of a slow, Southern drawl?

Before she could process that thought, or any thought at all actually, he slipped an arm around her and turned to smile at the two women who followed him onto the elevator. "See?" he said to them. "Here she is."

Both women were very New York, sleek and stunning, and…*laughing?* Whatever the man had been referring to, they weren't buying it. "Come on, Chef," one said, shaking her head.

Em stood there, not quite in shock, but not quite in charge of her faculties, either, because the man had her snug to his body, which she could feel was solid muscle, and warm, so very warm. Her head fit perfectly in the crook of his shoulder. At five foot nine she'd never fit into the crook of anyone's shoulder before, not a single one of her toads, and feeling—dare she think it?—petite and delicate made her want to sigh. The feminist in her tried to revolt, but was overpowered by her inner girlie-girl.

Then the man holding her tipped his face to hers. He

had a day's growth of dark stubble along his jaw, a silver stud in one ear and the darkest, thickest eyelashes she'd ever seen. He could convince a nun to sin with one crook of a finger, Em thought dazedly.

He was still smiling, only it wasn't a sweet, fuzzy smile but a purely mischievous, trouble-filled one.

My, Grandma, what big teeth you have. Really she needed to get herself together. But he was so yummy she hadn't yet decided whether to smack him or grab him. And then he leaned in, brushing that slightly rough jaw to her ear, the friction of his day's growth against her soft skin making her shiver.

"Do you mind?" he whispered, his voice low and husky. "If I kiss you?"

Kiss her? She wanted to have his firstborn!

"Just for show," he murmured, drawing her in closer as if she'd already agreed.

Em's mind raced. He didn't look like the toads she'd been with lately. He didn't feel like a toad. But would she ever really know unless she kissed him...?

No, it was crazy; it was beyond crazy, letting a perfect stranger touch her, much less *kiss* her, but something about his mocha eyes, about what she saw in them— places and experiences she'd never even dreamed about—made her let out a slow, if unsure, nod.

He rewarded her with a smile that finally met those eyes of his. And then he lowered his mouth.

The two women behind him, the ones who'd been laughing at him only a moment ago, both let out shocked gasps.

That was all Em heard before her mind shut itself off and became a simple recipient of sensations. His lips were firm yet soft, his breath warm and delicious, and on top of it all, the man smelled so good she could have inhaled him all day long.

As a result, her lips seemed to part by themselves, and at the unmistakable invitation, her prince let out a rough sound of surprise and deepened the kiss, his fingers massaging the back of her head at her nape, his other hand sliding down, down, *down*, coming to rest low on her spine, his fingers almost on her butt, anchoring her to him.

Oh, my.

And the kiss…it didn't make any sense. She didn't know him from Adam, but somehow she felt as if that weren't really true, as if maybe she'd always known him, as if her body recognized the connection even if her brain couldn't place him. Confusing, bewildering, but she held on to him as if it didn't matter. And he kept kissing her, kissing her until she felt hot everywhere, until she was making little sounds in the back of her throat that would have horrified her if she could have put together a single thought.

It was as if he knew the secret rhythm that her body's needs responded to, as if they'd been lovers before.

And yet it wasn't real. Logically Em knew this, even through the sensual, earthy haze he'd created, but it also seemed shockingly profound. And nothing, nothing at all, like a simple toad's kiss.

Then he lifted his head, her perfect stranger, and for one beat in time looked every bit as flummoxed as she.

But the moment passed and he smiled—a smile that was sin personified. She tried to respond in kind, she really did, but all she managed was to open her mouth, and quite possibly drool.

With one last stroke of his hand up her spine, a touch that conveyed a carefully restrained passion, he pulled his arm free, and when the elevator doors opened, he pushed his gaping friends off the elevator.

Then turned back to Em.

She stood there blinking like an owl, unable to shift her tongue from drool mode into talk mode.

"Thank you," he said.

Thank you?

"I'm in your debt." His voice was far tighter and more tense than it had been before the kiss. Interesting.

And then, just like that, the shockingly sexy, charismatic man walked away.

Still gaping, body still pulsing, Em became vaguely aware that the elevator doors closed again. Her heart pounded, her knees shook, and she stood there like a stunned possum until the elevator doors once again opened.

A few people got on.

At least she finally managed to close her mouth, then leaned back against the mirrors, happy for the support.

There was some talking around her but her brain couldn't process the words.

When the doors opened again, everyone got off and she had to laugh at herself.

She was back on the lobby floor.

"Get it together, Harris," she told herself, and even

hearing her voice seemed funny. She sounded shaky, a little off her axis.

A little? She'd fallen right off her world, that's what she'd done.

Shrugging, she once again hit the button for the twelfth floor, wondering when the doors had opened there and she'd missed it.

During the kiss?

Or after, when she'd been rendered a mass of sensual nerve endings incapable of doing anything but reacting?

Because of that kiss. The mother of all kisses. The kind of connection a woman dreamed about but was never really certain even existed, except in romance novels or the movies.

How did a man learn to kiss like that?

Given her reaction to it, that sort of ability should be registered as a lethal weapon.

And she didn't even know his name…

When the doors opened on the twelfth floor, *again*, she stopped hugging herself and stepped off, still in enough of a daze to do so without her roll-on luggage.

She ran back onto the elevator and grabbed her belongings.

Then she headed toward her room, unable to help but wonder if the rest of her trip was going to prove as adventurous as the first few minutes had been.

And that's when it came to her, what the women had called her glorious stranger.

They'd called him Chef.

To: Maintenance
From: Housekeeping
Check the air vents and temp regulator on elevator 2A. Guest seen coming out of it today looking dazed and flushed.

JACOB HILL walked through the employee quarters, located on the second sublevel. Employees were treated well at Hush, probably because the creator of the hotel, Piper Devon, was a genuine, caring people-person, no matter that the press liked to call her the original Paris Hilton. That was because they saw only a gorgeous blond trust-fund baby. But anyone who'd ever worked for Piper knew the truth. She worked her ass off, especially on Hush.

Jacob moved through the cafeteria toward the locker room. There he received a few whistles and catcalls, and when he got close to his locker, he saw why.

A pair of black satin panties hung off the lock.

"Another thong." Jon, one of the doormen, stood at the locker next to Jacob's, changing for his shift. He was young, in his early twenties, and staring at the panties as if they werc a choice cut New York steak. "It must be two times a week you get them," he said, bemused. "All I ever get is dumped."

Jacob gingerly removed the thong and tossed it to him. "Merry Christmas."

"Seriously, Chef, I want to know." Jon looked down at the satin in his hands. "What's your trick? I mean you get phone numbers, presents…give up the secret, man."

Jacob opened his locker and said nothing. There was nothing to say. After all, he didn't purposely do anything to gain women's attention—it just happened. A lot. He'd enjoyed it far more when he'd been young and stupid, when he'd happily worked his way through the line of women that had come his way.

He still enjoyed a woman's touch, her scent, her body, her everything, but lately, something had changed. He didn't seem to have quite the same patience for the game.

Was he getting old at thirty-four? Scary thought.

"I mean, I've done everything right," Jon said. "I call a woman when I say I'm going to. I listen to her ramble on and on and on. I take her dancing. I sweet-talk her."

Jacob grabbed his gear, shut his locker and then looked at Jon. "I'm going to sound like a first-class ass here, but the truth is…no. Never mind."

"Tell me. Whatever it is, I can do it."

"Okay, but listen. I should add a disclaimer here. I really don't recommend—"

"Dude. Just tell me."

"You're trying too hard."

The kid stared at Jacob. "Huh?"

"I know." Jacob lifted his hands. "It doesn't make any sense, but women seem to go for the guy who steps all over them, a guy who doesn't call, doesn't listen—"

"*That's* your secret?" Jon asked in disbelief. "Treat them like shit?"

Jacob shrugged. "I didn't say I condone it. I'm just giving you my observation."

"Wow." The young doorman stared down at the panties in his hands. "*Wow.*"

Jacob patted his shoulder and took the stairs back to the main level, entering the leaded glass doors of Amuse Bouche from the lobby.

Fresh flowers had been put out, as they were every day, making the place look warm and welcoming, and casually elegant. Unlike anywhere else, he never tired of being here, of the familiar black tables and funky black chairs bathed in the soft pink light, the gorgeous art deco paintings on the walls.

Inside his kitchen, he did as he always did—took a moment to survey his domain, the best money could buy in both design and appliances. No complaints here, either. The place had been cleaned during the wee hours of the night, to a spotless, disinfected, lemony-smelling shine that he never failed to marvel at. He could probably serve his food right here on this floor. Hell, he could probably serve out of their trash bin and still pass code, the place was so immaculate.

He marveled at that, too. There had been years when he would have happily eaten off this floor, or gone through the trash for scraps to fill his aching belly. Long, lean times, his growing-up years.

And now here he was, sous-chef of all things, reporting only to the executive chef who showed up on-site maybe once a week, leaving Jacob to handle the day-to-day operation of the place.

A slow, satisfied smile crossed his face. Not bad for a street urchin who'd grown up wild and feral, who'd wandered his way across the South in his youth, living hand to mouth, lucky to have a shirt on his back half the time. God, he'd been such a little shit, a real know-it-all. The one time that social services had managed to get hold of him, their diagnosis had been attachment disorder, which had cracked him up. Attachment disorder, bullshit. He could have attached. He'd just chosen not to.

Still did.

In any case, it was true that Amuse Bouche was everything he once would have scoffed at: posh and sophisticated, valuing quality over quantity. Odd then how very happy he was here, when his surroundings were far more elegant than he could ever be.

Ah, well. There it was. And eventually, he knew, the wanderlust would take over, as it always did, and he'd shrug and move on, never looking back.

But for now, things were pretty damn fine. He had all this incredible space, with the best equipment available, and the freshest ingredients money could buy. In a couple of hours' time the dining area would be filled with people wanting to taste his food. *His*.

Yeah, not too shabby, for a hard-ass punk kid from Podunk.

He moved toward the three industrial-grade refrigerators, thinking there were two things worth doing well in life. Both required passion, concentration and skill, and both gave him great pleasure: cooking and seducing a woman. Combining ingredients to create a masterpiece had always been a great source of entertainment. In the same way that the weather changed, without rhythm or plan, he liked to adjust his menu.

Women were no different. Same as a good recipe, they were meant to be played with, thoroughly explored, and devoured, but would undoubtedly spoil if kept too long.

So he never kept anything too long.

It simply wasn't in his nature. It was why he held the sous-chef position instead of executive chef, which he could have had if he wanted.

He didn't want.

He liked keeping his options open, liked keeping one foot out the door, liked knowing he could pack up and go at a moment's notice.

Hell, he didn't even have to pack if he wanted, he had nothing that couldn't be replaced in another town, another restaurant.

But for now, for right this very minute, Hush was a good place to be. A very good place. He smiled as he remembered the episode in the elevator, with his pretty stranger and her mind-blowing kiss.

"What are you grinning about?" This came from Pru as she entered into the kitchen behind him. She was

Amuse Bouche's sommelier. The wine expert position fit his friend to a tee, given that she was a complete snob and had been since her first day here, even though, like Jacob, she'd arrived in New York with only the clothes on her back.

But she was extremely sharp-witted, and never failed to amuse him. They'd bonded immediately, of course, recognizing kindred spirits. The two pretenders, they called themselves.

Oddly enough, they hadn't slept together.

A first for Jacob, being friends with a woman, not lovers. But though Pru, with her curvy, lush body, creamy porcelain skin and startlingly blue eyes, was exactly his type on paper, in reality she batted for another team entirely.

An all-girl team.

After the initial disappointment, Jacob hadn't cared. He liked her, and that in itself was enough of a novelty that he put up with her less attractive traits—such as the one that made her get some sick enjoyment out of constantly trying to set him up with "the one."

The one. Why did there have to be just one?

"Do I need a reason to be grinning?" he asked.

"Yeah, when you're smirking like that." Pru studied him thoughtfully, her dark brown hair carefully contained in some complicated braid. "You're thinking about sex."

He laughed. *Caught.* "Why do you always assume that?"

"Because guys think about sex 24/7. You're probably

thinking about that poor woman you accosted in the elevator."

"I didn't accost her." Nope, after a brief startled moment on her part, she'd kissed him back. Quite eagerly.

"Who was she?"

A stranger, one who happened to be at the right place at the right time. A stranger by whom, for those sixty or so seconds, he'd been transfixed. As for who she was, he had no idea. He could have found out, of course, but it had been just a kiss.

Just a helluva kiss.

"My date."

Pru set down her Prada briefcase, overflowing with wine catalogs and food magazines, and put her hands on her hips. "You don't really expect me to believe she was your date."

"Why not?"

"Because she looked too sweet to have slept with you."

She *had* looked sweet in that long, flowery dress that had hugged her curves in a way that had made his mouth water. Sweet and yet hot. Extremely hot. "I don't sleep with all my first dates."

Pru laughed. "Yes, you do."

"I didn't sleep with you."

"In your dreams you did," she said smugly.

Okay, she had him there, and he had to laugh. "I'm not that big of a slut."

"Honey, if the shoe fits…" She pulled a California winery brochure from her bag, tapping the label with a perfectly manicured finger. "We want their stuff."

He glanced at the cover, which showed wine country in all its fall glory. "What makes it different?"

"You'll have to taste it. It's out of this world. I want to make an order. All right with you?"

"You know I trust you."

"Uh-huh," she said dryly. "Which is why you date only the women I tell you to."

"Correction. I trust your judgment in *wines.*"

"I have great taste in women." Pru waggled her brow. "I'm going to find you the right one yet, you'll see."

"We've been over this, Pru."

"I know, I know. The thought of just one woman makes you shudder, yadda, yadda. That's only because you don't know, Jacob. You don't understand how great it can be."

The kitchen doors slammed open and another woman entered. Tall, willowy, olive-skinned and gorgeous, Caya was part of the waitstaff, and Pru's platonic room-mate. If Pru was the sedate and elegant lady, Caya was the happy-go-lucky party girl. The perfect odd couple.

Caya divided a glance between the two of them. "Having a fiesta without me?"

"Just reminding Chef of all his faults," Pru told her.

"Hey, now." Caya slid her arms around Jacob, setting her head on his shoulder. "Silly Pru. Our Chef has no faults."

Jacob laughed. "That's right, I don't. And don't either of you forget it."

"We were talking about the elevator scene," Pru told Caya. "The woman."

"No, *you* were talking about it." Jacob opened the meat refrigerator and pulled out a container of fresh mussels.

"So." Caya leaned back against the counter and watched him. "You going to tell us?"

"Sure." Jacob dumped the mussels into a huge pot and carried it to the sink. "I'm creating an island blue mussel with sweet potato chowder." He began to fill the pot with water. "I've had a lot of requests—"

"Not *that*, you very annoying man." Pru moved close. "Although an excellent choice," she murmured, peering into the pot. "You should serve a light to medium-bodied off-dry wine with that, you know. Maybe even a lightly sweet white, like a Chenin Blanc or Vouvray—"

"Oh, my God, Pru," Caya said with a laugh. "Stop being the workaholic for a minute. Let's stick to the subject, okay? The cutie in the elevator?"

"Forget it. He can't tell you anything because he was just kissing some stranger again."

Jacob rolled his eyes.

"By the way, I met this woman in the spa today," Pru said to him. "I was getting a Swedish massage—which by the way, was *heaven*. Anyway, she'd be perfect for you."

Jacob lifted up the heavy pot of mussels. "You know, I see your lips moving, but all I hear is blah blah blah blah blah."

"Funny."

"I thought so."

"Jacob—"

"Hey, how about this? When you're not single, we'll talk." He carried the pot to the huge stovetop. "Meanwhile, go find 'the one.'"

He saw Pru's quick longing glance at Caya— Caya?—but before he could assimilate it, the door opened and Jacob's two assistants entered.

Timothy and Daniel had been picked by him personally, and after going through at least ten previous assistants, each worthless, he had high hopes for these two. They were clueless, of course, and both far too young, but he'd been young and stupid once, too, and since they had a genuine love of cooking and were eager to learn, he'd given them a shot.

Timothy leaned over Jacob's shoulder, looked into the pot and let out a slow smile. "Island blue mussels. *Sweet.*"

"It will be," Jacob promised. "Get out the whole dried bay laurel leaf and the coriander. Oh, and the fennel seed. Start grinding." To Daniel he said, "Get what we need for the soup. You know the ingredients?"

Daniel looked excited and terrified at the same time. "Yes."

"Then go. Oh, and stir frequently." He leaned in. "That means often, whether your girlfriend calls you every three minutes or not."

Daniel blushed at the reminder of last week, when he'd inadvertently burned the bottom of the pot and ruined an entire batch. "I won't screw it up this time."

"See that you don't."

"I was thinking," Caya piped up to Jacob. "We should all go out tonight."

By "all," Caya could mean anyone and everyone. While Pru batted for that all-girl's team, Caya had never limited her options by choosing a side.

"I'll bring that woman from the spa for Jacob," Pru said.

"Don't bother, I'm busy tonight," Jacob told her, and before they could object, he put an arm around each of them, steering them toward the door.

Laughing, Pru dug in her heels. "You are not busy."

"I am *extremely* busy."

"Fine. I can easily party without you guys," Caya said breezily.

At the flash of disappointment on Pru's face, Jacob sighed. Ah, hell. The Ice Queen had a thing for the carefree, spirited Caya, who went through sexual partners like water. Not that there was anything wrong with that, but Pru was the monogamous sort, always in it for the long haul. She'd been dreaming of her own special "the one" since he'd known her.

And now she was bound for Hurt City. "Maybe we could go out," Pru said to Caya. "You know, just the two of us."

Caya stared at her, then laughed. "Right. The sommelier go out with the lowly waitress. That's sweet, Pru, but you don't have to do that." Leaning in, she kissed each of them on the cheek. "See ya later, guys."

With that, she took her most excellent behind out of the kitchen.

Pru watched her leave the kitchen and Jacob shook his head. "Pru, what the hell is this?"

Pru swiped all expression from her face. "What?"

"You were looking at her."

"So? I was looking at you, too."

"Yes, but not like you wanted to lap me up with a spoon."

Pru reached for her briefcase and, taking a page from his own book, said nothing.

Jacob shook his head. "You should just come right out and tell her."

"Tell her what? There's nothing to tell."

Her face was pure stubbornness, and after a second, Jacob lifted his hands. "Fine."

"Fine." Pru left, too, shutting the door just a little too hard behind her.

Jacob shrugged it off and strode back toward his waiting ingredients with the same anticipation he would have had striding toward a woman in his bed.

3

EM, ERIC AND LIZA looked up as Amuse Bouche's maître d' came toward them. "We can seat you now," she said with an easy smile.

Amuse Bouche turned out to be casually elegant and extremely eye pleasing, with slender black urns holding arrangements of a variety of flowers that matched the art deco vibe of the rest of the hotel. The tables were well spaced and gorgeously done, each with its own discreet partition, so that while voices and laughter were audible, there was an illusion of intimacy for each party.

Em could use some privacy to obsess over what she thought of as the E.I.—elevator incident. Not going to happen with Eric and Liza just behind her, side by side and yet ignoring each other—well, if ignoring meant staring and pretending not to be.

Granted, Liza looked amazing in a tiny scrap of a red cocktail dress, which probably accounted for the glazed look on Eric's face. He didn't look too shabby in his finery, either, turning the head of more than one woman.

"Here you go," the maître d' said and gestured to their

table. "Tonight you'll be experiencing Chef Jacob Hill's renowned cuisine creations. Enjoy."

"I'm starving," Liza said and lifted her menu, which she used as a shield so she could covertly stare at Eric with the unguarded longing she sometimes got in her eyes.

Eric got the same look while pretending to watch the crowd, though really checking out the long length of Liza's bare, smooth legs.

It drove Em crazy—how could they not see they belonged together? *Everyone* knew it.

Everyone but them.

Em didn't look at her menu yet. She was still trying to find her own balance, and while she did, she looked around, too. Each place inside Hush had turned out to be more exciting and different than the last, full of a spirited energy and yet somehow also a Zen-like peace.

Not much of a hotel person herself, this one had won her over. Her room was large by Manhattan standards. Beach inspired, it was done in creamy blues and greens and earth tones, with a mural of the sun rising over the Atlantic on one wall, and a mounted waterfall on the other, giving off the soothing sounds of water running over rocks. Her California king bed had lush, thick bedding she couldn't have afforded at home, and her bathroom came with a huge sunken hot tub she could happily drown in, with scented candles lining the edges. The towels were Egyptian cotton, and on the counters had been lotions, bath oils, scrubs—a virtual day spa.

There had been more, as well: the TV channels that were exclusive to the hotel and showed an array of erotica, the beautifully illustrated copy of the Kama Sutra and a selection of self-heating lubricating oils in the bedside table. But the coup de grâce…in the tall closet outside the bathroom hung a long, intricately braided leather whip. She'd fingered the thing in amused shock, had even tapped it against her palm.

Ouch.

Em would have called herself sexually adventurous. Okay, maybe not quite, but she was at least sexually game. Now she had to admit, maybe she wasn't nearly as game as she'd thought.

This hotel had certainly been an eye-opener. A costly one. She thought of her expense account and winced as she stared at the elaborate but somehow elegantly simple, menu of Amuse Bouche. And yet, she reasoned, if coming here got her Chef Jacob Hill, then every penny spent would be worth its weight in gold.

Or so she hoped.

Logically she knew that even if she somehow managed the miracle and convinced him to come to Hollywood to star in his own TV show, it was only half the battle.

She still had a successful show to make.

One crisis at a time.

Liza set down her menu, took one look at Em and nodded. "Alcohol," she said. "We need some."

"Not until I talk to him," Em said, determined, but getting nervous. "I need all my wits about me for that."

"Honey, with this guy there's no chance of having your wits at all. The guy'll charm the pants right off you without trying."

"You don't know that."

"I've heard. And then what happened today proves it."

Em was already regretting that she'd told her friend about the E.I.

Liza waggled her carefully waxed eyebrows. "Personally, I think you should go for it, you could use the cookie."

"Cookie?"

"Orgasm," Eric explained, checking into the conversation. "She calls orgasms 'cookies'. She thinks it's cute."

"*You* used to think it was cute," Liza sniffed.

Eric's blue eyes sparkled. "Maybe I still do."

Liza stared at him, then reached for her water as if parched. Em eyed the door to the kitchen. "What's the best way to approach him, do you think?"

Liza was still staring at Eric. With what looked like great effort, she tore her gaze from him, her thumb rubbing her ring finger where her wedding band used to be. She turned to Em. "What did Nathan suggest?"

Nathan wanted her to play hardball from the start, offering Jacob standard money, and when he balked, adding small slices of the profits. And when all else failed, she was to resort to hair in the food.

As if she'd ever really do such a thing. "Maybe I could ask the waitress if I could talk to him."

"Jeez, at these prices, he oughta come with the meal. Maybe sing and dance, too." Eric tossed down his menu and smiled as the waitress came close. "Excuse me, do you know the chef?"

"Of course." The waitress smiled back. "Wait until you taste his food, it's out of this world."

Liza leaned close to Em. "And according to you, his food isn't the only thing that tastes out of this world."

"Stop." Em felt the blush creep up her face.

The waitress rattled off the specials. "Everything is fabulous. Trust me, you'll love everything you taste."

"Including the chef himself," Liza murmured for Em's ears only.

"Could we have another minute before deciding?" Em asked the waitress.

"Oh, you bet. Take your time."

Em waited until it was just them and turned to Liza. "I shouldn't have told you about the elevator incident. I don't even know for certain that it was him."

"Well, it was somebody named Chef. You sure you don't know *why* he kissed you?"

"No, he just said 'do you mind?' and then he was doing it."

"And you didn't think about kneeing him in the 'nads?" Eric asked.

At the first taste of him, Em hadn't thought at all. In fact, she'd been the one to deepen the connection. "It wasn't like that."

"Uh-huh." Liza looked at her speculatively. "Must have been some kiss."

Oh, yeah. "It was…interesting."

"Interesting? Honey, this menu is interesting. The

decor is interesting. But a kiss? A kiss is either hot stuff or not worth the trouble. No in-between."

Worth the trouble. Times ten. Times infinity.

Eric was studying Liza thoughtfully. "Which was it with us?"

"What?"

"Those two months we were married. Was it hot stuff or not worth the trouble?"

Liza opened her mouth, then closed it.

Eric's amusement faded, replaced by an unmistakable hurt. "Right."

The waitress came back and took their orders by memory, and then offered the services of their sommelier, who could come to the table and make wine suggestions if they'd like.

The sommelier turned out to be one of the women in the elevator, though if the tall, elegant, beautiful brunette recognized Em, she gave no indication of it.

When they were alone again, Liza set down her drink and looked at Eric. "It was hot stuff."

Now it was Eric's turn to blink in surprise.

Liza seemed just as taken aback and abruptly turned to Em. "If you don't approach the chef tonight you'll have to make an appointment," she babbled. "By all accounts, this guy is media reclusive, and not interested in a career path other than what suits him personally. I bet he wouldn't easily grant you an interview."

"I know." Em had worried about this. She worried about a lot of things. But mostly facing the sexy, gorgeous Jacob Hill now that she knew he lived up to his reputation. "I need to make contact tonight—" She broke off when the waitress came back and set down a plate of appetizers that they hadn't ordered.

"From the chef," the woman explained. "Vegetable spring rolls with chili oil and teriyaki mustard sauce. They're a favorite here."

Eric looked around at the other tables. They were all filled with people having conversations, sharing food, all enjoying themselves greatly, if the happy buzz in the place meant anything. "Does the chef always give away his food?"

"For his friends, or special guests, yes."

Liza looked at Em.

So did Eric.

Em laughed nervously. "Uh, thank you."

"Enjoy."

"Oh, boy," Em whispered when she'd left. "Do you think he sees us here?"

"*You*, you mean," Liza said. "Does he see *you* here. Of course he does. He sent the food over."

Em stared at the appetizers, then looked around her. Waitstaff moved easily and discreetly around the crowded room. No chef in sight.

"Must have been a helluva kiss." Liza dug into the spring rolls, then moaned. "Oh, my God. Em, you've got to taste this."

"Oh, yeah," Eric said when he'd popped one in his mouth. "This guy knows his stuff."

"The man's a god," Liza moaned.

"Are you sure all you did was kiss him, Em?" Eric

reached for his second. "Because this isn't a thank-you for a kiss. This is a thank-you for a good fu—"

"Eric." Liza glared at him.

Eric just popped another appetizer into his mouth.

"Men," Liza muttered. "Dogs."

"Woof woof," he agreed happily.

Em shook her head and tasted a roll herself. It did melt in her mouth, made her stomach rumble happily, and actually brought a helpless smile to her face, just as a movement caught the corner of her eye.

A tall, broad man stood at the back of the restaurant, leaning against the doorjamb of the kitchen. Seeming extremely comfortable with both himself and his sur-roundings, his posture and manner spoke of a quiet, rock-solid confidence.

A confidence she'd experienced firsthand.

Unlike earlier in the elevator, he wore a white chef's hat and jacket, which only accentuated to his height and well-built body. His staff moved around him like a well-tuned army, most of them taking the time to say something to him, or at least cast him a smile, which he always returned.

"That's him?" Liza whispered. "Because *wow*."

"Yeah." Suddenly Em felt hot in the cool room, and reached for her water. Even from this distance she felt the weight of his quiet, assessing stare, and wondered what he was thinking.

Then his lips curved oh-so-slightly, and she knew.

He was thinking about the kiss, the one that would have knocked her socks off if she'd been wearing any, the one that had rendered her deaf, dumb and blind.

And made her wet.

Even now, her thighs tightened with the memory, and she squirmed.

And his not-quite-smile went just a bit naughty.

Oh, God. Her glass nearly slipped out of her hand, and she set it down with such awkwardness on the table that water sloshed over the edge.

"Easy," Liza murmured, putting a hand over hers. Then she smiled at the chef, pointing to the appetizers, and gave him the thumbs-up sign.

Chef smiled and gave a slight nod of his head.

Nope, no trouble in the confidence arena.

"He is pretty yummy," Liza noted, and Eric craned his neck to check him out.

"Not that yummy," he said.

Liza laughed and patted Eric's arm. "Don't worry. You're yummy, too."

"Yeah?" He turned a suddenly extremely interested face toward her. "You still think so, huh?"

Liza shrugged. "You have a mirror."

He grinned and leaned in close. "If I'm so yummy, why did you let me go?"

They all knew why. Because Liza's crappy childhood memories of her mother's eight marriages had made her afraid of commitment.

Eric, who'd grown up without a mother at all, had the same issue. Together, they hadn't trusted their love enough, and they'd had two collective feet halfway out the door at all times.

Now Liza, more mature in many ways, strove to keep

it light and tapped him playfully on the nose. "I let you go because you're an ass."

"Yeah, maybe, but I'm a yummy ass." Eric grabbed her hand and ran his thumb over her bare ring finger. "Now tell me the truth. Why did you let me go?"

"An ass is an ass, Eric."

"Right." Eric nodded, and sat back. "That explains it. Clear as mud, thanks."

Across the room, the sommelier handed the chef a champagne bottle and gestured to a table. Jacob Hill nodded, then walked over to the couple seated there, where he began conversing with them as he smoothly, easily, opened their champagne for them.

"Just look at him," Liza murmured. "Do you suppose he makes love to a woman the same way he opens a bottle of champagne? I bet he does."

Em thought about that and felt her body heat up even more.

The waitress set their dishes on the table, momentarily blocking Em's view of the other table. By the time she moved away, Jacob Hill was gone.

She didn't see him again during the scrumptious meal during which the three of them shared two bottles of wine. They turned down dessert and once they'd settled the bill, Liza stood up first and visibly wobbled.

Eric surged up and slid an arm around her. "Whoa there, tiger."

Liza grinned and set her head on his shoulder. "You're so pretty."

Brow raised, Eric looked at Em.

"Three glasses of wine," Em explained.

"That's right. I'm a cheap drunk." Liza grinned, sliding her hand down Eric's back to pinch his butt.

Eric narrowed his eyes. "What was *that?*"

She waggled her brow. "What did it feel like?"

Eric shook his head. "You are *not* coming on to me."

"Okay, I'm not." She laughed and patted the butt she'd just pinched. "But I am," she whispered extremely loudly.

"You said you'd rot in hell before you slept with me again," he said, confused.

"Silly man." She went to pat his cheek, missed, and nearly poked out his eye. "Never take a PMSing woman seriously."

"Okay." Eric caught her hand, saving his other eye, and nodding agreeably as he pulled her close. "I can work with this information."

"Eric. She's tipsy," Em admonished. "You can't take advantage of a tipsy woman."

"Sure he can." Liza bit his throat, eliciting a rough sound from Eric. "Take advantage of me all you want."

Eric let out another sound, this one of regret. "Em's right. Knock it off."

"Fine. I'll go to my room," Liza said. "Where I plan to eat everything in the minibar. Did you see that thing? It's completely stocked with stuff from Dean & Deluca."

"You just ate," Eric reminded her.

Liza waggled a finger in his face, this time almost poking it up his nose. "Do you know nothing of women?"

"Apparently not."

"Just take me to my bed, superhero."

Eric's eyes darkened. "I like the super part."

"Eric," Em warned softly.

"Right." He frowned at Liza. "I'll put you to bed, but that's all I'm doing."

"Oooh, playing hard to get." Liza sighed and again set her head to his chest, staring up at him adoringly. "You're good at that."

Eric looked over her head at Em helplessly.

She shook her head.

Eric's jaw ticked. "I'll get her to her room. You going to be okay here by yourself?"

"I'll be safer than you," Em assured him, watching as he led Liza out of the restaurant.

Alone, Em looked around her and decided if she sat for much longer, she'd just begin obsessing again. Maybe instead, she'd walk around the city for a little bit to clear her head. Make a plan of action that involved more than drooling after the man she needed to talk into saving her sorry butt.

She got as far as standing up and reaching for her purse when a low, husky voice drawled in her ear, "Leaving without dessert is an insult to the chef."

Her heart kicked once hard, and she turned her head, coming eye to chest with Chef Jacob Hill. At the sight of him, the rest of her kicked. The man exuded a raw sexuality that made her feel her own sexuality in ways she hadn't in a long time, if ever. "You."

"Me," he agreed. "You look beautiful."

"Oh…thank you." She tugged at her black cocktail

dress, modestly cut, but snug and—she hoped—relatively sexy. "I wasn't sure of the dress code here—"

"I didn't mean your clothes." When he smiled, as he did now with a dash of wicked intent, he flashed a single dimple on his right cheek, and she had the sudden, shocking urge to run a fingertip over the spot.

He hadn't shaved, and the slight stubble on his jaw was nearly longer than the short hair on his head. She wondered if it would be soft to the touch, then wondered why she wondered.

Because she was losing her mind, that was why.

He was younger than she'd imagined, but there was something about the way he held himself, and the way he took her in, that spoke of a much older soul. His mile-long legs were encased in black trousers instead of his Levi's, his feet in much cleaner, much newer black boots than the ones he'd had on in the elevator.

Chef Jacob Hill cleaned up real nice.

"Crème brûlée or white peach cobbler?" he asked. "Or maybe a cheese plate with an imported selection of artisanal?"

She slid her hand to her belly, which was jumping nervously. *Ask him. Ask him to be your TV chef.* She was afraid if she opened her mouth she was going to ask him something else entirely.

Come to my bed.

"I'm full."

"Are you kidding? You're never too full for dessert."

His voice was somehow extremely arousing, which

she told herself would be great for the show, and that was why she'd noticed.

A lie.

She'd noticed because she was a woman. A woman who'd felt his voice all the way to her toes. In fact, the tingling effect began deep in her womb and spread, and she squirmed some more.

He noticed. His eyes cut to her body as she wiggled, and then back up to her gaze, something new there besides the curiosity and wry amusement.

Heat. Lots of heat.

Oh, boy. Resisting the urge to fan cool air in front of her hot face, she searched around for something else to lock her gaze on, for something to occupy her mind, because ever since that elevator kiss, nothing else but this man had.

The tables were all hopping with activity, everyone enjoying themselves. Waiters and waitresses moved around, serving with easy charm and personality, all so beautiful Em could have hired any one of them for her show and the cameras would have been thrilled.

One particularly beautiful waitress was serving a table of elderly gentlemen with professionalism, even when the oldest of the bunch reached out and patted her butt.

In return she shook her head and patted the top of his head with a smile. The old man adjusted his toupee and smiled with only a hint of regret.

Oh, good. *Everyone* had sex on the brain, not just Em. Maybe it was the hotel. She reached for her water and gulped it down.

"You okay?" he asked her, bringing her attention back to him.

As if she could possibly forget he was there.

Not quite sure she trusted herself to speak, she nodded her head. *See? See how fine I am? And by the way, will you come with me to Hollywood and save my sorry career?*

"Please, sit," he urged, putting a hand on her arm.

Just like in the elevator, his touch electrified.

"I'd really love to bring you dessert," he said. He smiled a little. Could he see how he turned her on without even trying? "I owe you."

"No, that's okay. Really. I—"

He put a finger on her lips, yet again touching her, and yet again causing her every hormone to stand up and take notice.

"Wait here," he said in quiet demand.

Wait here, repeated those hormones, and quivered. She nodded, and he gave her another little knowing smile that told her he realized exactly what he did to her. She watched him stride off, tall, sure...confident that she'd wait simply because he'd commanded it to be so.

She didn't understand it, but he had this unsettling way about him of getting her to do what he wanted.

What was that?

She had no idea, but she waited. But only because she wanted to.

4

HE'D MADE HER SQUIRM, Jacob thought, intrigued. He walked into the restaurant kitchen, grabbed a plate and loaded it himself, intending on sitting with her to watch her eat, and to see if he could make her squirm again because it was damned arousing.

She was arousing, with her wide, expressive eyes, her full lips that she kept licking nervously. Her voice. Her taste. The way she looked at him. As if he was some forbidden treat tempting her to the ends of her restraints.

He moved back into the dining area, which was filled with contented diners, and felt that same surge of fulfillment he got every single night. She was still sitting there, watching him approach with both wariness and something else, something he recognized well. Awareness.

Let the dance begin, he thought, and smiled as he sat. "Try this. Bouche S'mores. House-made marshmallow, fresh graham crackers and imported semisweet chocolate, all melted over an open flame."

"House-made marshmallow?"

"Yes." He met her gaze. "We get a lot of requests for marshmallows via room service, melted of course."

She stared down at the plate, a lovely flush working up her cheeks.

"People are very fond of melted marshmallow," he said. "Specifically, they're fond of licking them."

She gave a slow blink. "Oh. Um—"

"Off of each other," he clarified. "Not the plate."

She reached out to touch the stack of marshmallow. Felt the soft, warm, gooey texture. She cocked her head as if considering exactly how to lick it off another person and, just like that, the tables turned, and Jacob was the one squirming.

"Interesting," she said, throwing him further off balance. "Seems a bit fattening, but I'm sure it's worth it." She bit her lower lip, each of her thoughts chasing another across her face.

She was picturing it. With *him*.

He sank a fork into his fun creation and leaned across the table, touching the marshmallow to her lips. She opened her mouth, tongue darting out to catch a dollop.

Their gazes locked, and when she moaned in delight at the taste, he nearly moaned, too, at the look of rapture on her face.

"Delicious," she said when she'd swallowed. "But I have a feeling you already know it."

Ah. She was quiet but not shy, and that in itself was another unexpected turn-on. "Yes. I know it." When she laughed, he decided he liked the sweet, musical sound because it wasn't silly, it wasn't fake. It was real.

She was real, and damn if he didn't want to know more about her.

"I don't even know who you are," she murmured, clearly having some of the same thoughts. "And yet here we sit, discussing your marshmallows and their incredibly diverse uses here at the hotel."

A conversation he most definitely wanted to have, but... "You don't know who I am?"

She slid him a self-deprecatory smile. "Okay, so you're Chef Jacob Hill."

"Which leaves me at a disadvantage."

She smiled. "I doubt you're ever at a disadvantage."

He laughed and relaxed, realizing his instincts had been right. He was going to enjoy himself with her, immensely. "What's your name?"

"Emmaline Harris. Television producer."

"Emmaline," he repeated, liking the way her name rolled off his tongue. "Are you enjoying your stay here at Hush?"

She seemed surprised that he hadn't jumped on her profession. But they were nothing if not discreet here at Hush, where they hosted celebrities and movie stars all the time, and she guessed he wouldn't bring it up again unless she did.

"Yes, I'm enjoying myself," she said. "It's very lovely here."

Lovely. Not a word he'd have used to describe the more adventurous and eclectic services the hotel had to offer, which meant she was either being coy, or she hadn't experienced any of it. "Are you staying for business or pleasure?"

At the word pleasure, her tongue darted out again and nervously licked her lips. "Business."

"That's a shame."

She laughed, a little nervously now. "Yes."

It should have given him pause that he'd flustered her, but instead, it excited him. He was thinking of all the ways he could fluster her some more when she spoke again.

"I'm here to find the next new reality TV star."

Reality TV. The genre appealed to him about as much as a trip to the dentist. "Hmm."

"You don't like reality TV?" she asked.

"Actually, I'm not into any kind of TV," he admitted. "Not my thing."

"What about if you could be on it?" she asked. She was watching him carefully. "On your own show."

"Sounds like a nightmare."

"Oh." She looked at him for a long moment, assessing for God knew what. Speculating on the mysteries of the female mind was always a bit like tiptoeing through a minefield. "Tell me something," she said. "Do you kiss every strange woman you meet in the elevator?"

"Ah." He'd been waiting for her to broach the subject. "That."

"You must have known we'd have to talk about it."

He lifted a shoulder.

"What if I'd been married?" she asked. "Or attached?"

"Are you?"

"No."

"Then no harm, no foul."

"Is that a life motto for you?"

"Pretty much." He smiled.

She returned it, but he could still see the wheels spinning. Her eyes were clear on his, such a mossy, pretty green. The rest of her was pretty, too. Shoulder-length brown wavy hair with long choppy bangs that she kept shoving out of her eyes, a narrow strong face, with a most lovely mouth, as he had reason to know. She had good height on her—another bonus for him at six foot four—and plenty of curves, he was happy to note. He didn't approve of skinny.

"Why did you do it?" she asked, taking another bite of the s'mores, which meant that while she might be a tad shy, she went after what she wanted. He liked that. "Why did you kiss me?" she pressed.

"Because I wanted to."

She laughed, and took another bite. "Do you always do whatever you want?"

He thought about that. "Mostly."

"There was another reason you kissed me," she insisted.

"Okay, yes."

She waited, a brow raised.

"You see, I have these two extremely nosy, bossy, interfering people in my life," he admitted. "They're very annoying."

"Then why are they in your life?"

He sighed. "They're my friends."

That wrangled a laugh out of her. "Okay, I'll buy that. I have two of those myself."

"They think because I'm single that I need to be fixed. In their mind, that fixing requires a woman."

"So? You're a big boy. Say no."

He smiled. "Tell me something, Emmaline."

"Em," she said softly, staring at his mouth as if maybe she liked his smile.

He hoped so, because he liked hers, very much. "Em, then." Yeah, that suited her even better. Em was even softer, more feminine. It fit her to a tee. Which didn't explain why he wanted to sit here with her all night. "You ever successfully say no to the people in your life?"

"I'm a sucker when it comes to the people I care about."

Why the hell *that* attracted him, too, he had no idea. "Exactly."

She was still shaking her head. "You're no one's sucker, Jacob Hill."

"No, I'm not. But I still care about my friends."

Her eyes softened. "That's very sweet."

"Actually, I'm the furthest thing from sweet you've ever met."

Her gaze searched his for a long moment, while all around them the restaurant continued to buzz with life—talking, laughing, music. There were a few celebrities here tonight, as well: a big movie star, and also a national newscaster, both being left alone thanks to his discreet staff. There was also a rock star at the center table, *not* being left alone, but then he'd come here to be noticed and fawned over. The guy undoubtedly had his pick of the women here tonight.

Emmaline kept her gaze locked on Jacob's. "Something's not adding up."

"What?"

"Why would you need to be set up?" The moment the words left her mouth, she looked embarrassed. "It's just that you don't look like you'd need any help in that area."

"Thank you."

"Actually, I didn't mean it as a compliment."

He grinned. Yeah, he liked her. "My friend Pru, the sommelier who helped you pick out your wine, she thinks I need to experience a 'real' relationship. That's because hers have all been so important to her—she's convinced I'm missing out by not experiencing that."

Em shook her head. "See, now this should be in the friendship handbook. When you fall in love, you should be required to contain your happiness and not try to spread it around."

"No one's in love."

"Your friend...."

He was shaking his head.

"What was she doing in *her* 'real' relationship then?"

"Having lots of sex, I imagine."

Her brows vanished beneath her bangs. "So you both have something against love?"

"I didn't say I did."

"You didn't have to. It was in your tone."

He just eyed her while she smiled at him, seeming quite amused at his expression. "So we've just discovered something you *don't* do," she said thoughtfully. "That's good, actually. I'm relieved to find out you're not perfect."

A shocked laugh escaped him. How long had it been since someone challenged him? Too long, if this was giving him a thrill. "I have a thing against the way people fling the love word around," he said, knowing this area was a deal breaker for most women, who wholeheartedly bought into the love myth, to the point that it tainted their every date.

Not him. There wasn't a single dab of naiveté or innocence left in him, and he hadn't believed in something as elusive and unattainable as the Easter Bunny or love since he was four years old. Truth was truth. Love was nothing but a big, fat pain in the ass. "I'll tell you one thing," he said.

"And what's that?"

"The night's too good to waste it philosophizing on some emotion that may or may not exist."

"True enough."

He had to get back to the kitchen. They both knew it, and yet Jacob wanted to stall longer, keep her talking. Or at least smiling at him like that.

But she pushed her now-empty plate away. "That was heavenly. Thank you so much."

When she stood, he did as well, taking her hand and bringing it up to his mouth. "Have a great night," he murmured, his lips against her skin.

She looked up into his eyes, hers a little dazed as she shook her head. "You're probably the only man I know who could pull off that ridiculously romantic gesture."

Lightly he scraped his teeth against her knuckles, taking the "romantic gesture" straight into raw sexual mode. He noted her sharp inhale. "Enjoy your stay," he said softly, and let her pull her hand free.

Still staring at him, she brought her hand up to her cheek, the movement oddly tender and vulnerable. But instead of feeling as if he had the upper hand as she turned and walked off into the hotel, he felt as if he needed to sit down.

Or touch her again.

EM TOOK THE ELEVATOR without incident. Meaning no gorgeous stranger stepped on, pulled her into his arms and kissed her senseless.

She told herself the vague disappointment in her gut was about the cooking program. He'd said the thought of being on his own show sounded like a nightmare.

God. What now? When the doors opened on the twelfth floor, she looked down the hall at her door, decided she wasn't ready to be alone and headed toward Liza's room instead. Hopefully Eric had gotten her tucked safely into bed and—

And Eric was sitting on the floor right outside Liza's room, head back against the door, looking miserable.

"Eric?" She crouched before him and took his hand in hers. "Honey, what's the matter?"

"Nothing." His smile didn't reach his eyes. "I tucked her in. She's out like a light. Did you know she snores?"

"Like a buzz saw. But what are you still doing here?"

"I…" Closing his eyes, he lightly thunked his head

back against the door. "Nothing. Never mind." He rose to his feet. "'Night."

She caught his arm before he got away. "Eric."

He shoved his fingers through his hair, tousling the golden ends. "I brought her up here intending to…" Now he scrubbed a hand over his face. "I wanted to…"

"I know." She laid a hand on his arm. "But she was drunk. You did the right thing by walking away, no matter how much in love with her you still are."

Eric's gaze flew to hers. "I'm not…"

Em just looked at him.

"I'm really not…"

Em smiled gently and stroked her hand up his tense arm.

"*Shit*," he said. "I am. Tell me she doesn't know."

"Are you kidding? Our Liza? She's pretty much only thinking about her own feelings at the moment."

"Yeah." He sighed. "She couldn't even get out of her clothes—she insisted I unzip her dress. Then the little fool tripped over it and I had to—" He groaned, walked down the hallway and stalked back. "I had to strip her down and shove her into that bed, and the whole time she was teasing me, asking me if I wanted to kiss her, touch her—"

"She was drunk," she reminded him softly. "She didn't mean to be a tease."

"Yes, she did."

"Okay, well, she didn't mean to be cruel about it."

"Which is the only reason I didn't—" He scrunched up his face. "*God.* She's going to be the death of me."

"Have you thought about telling her how you feel?"

"Oh, yeah." He laughed harshly. "That'd go over well. I'm the one who cried uncle and walked, remember? I can't tell her now. She'd just use it against me."

"I think you're wrong." She hugged him. "Look, if you can't handle this trip, I totally understand." She needed him, but his happiness meant a lot to her. "You can fly home and I'll—"

"I can handle this." He straightened with great resolve. "Trust me, I can handle this."

"If you're sure—"

"Very. Did you get the chef tonight?"

"Uh…not yet. Soon. Just get some sleep, okay?"

"Yeah. 'Night."

She went to her room and sighed at the glorious beach-themed decor that instantly instilled her with a sense of calm peace.

Or would have if tonight had gone off the way it should have.

She kicked off her shoes, her toes sinking inches into the opulent carpet. If she had to be stressed, at least this was a damn fine place to do it. After stripping, she took a long bath in her hot tub, and though she didn't mean to, she stared at the flickering candles and let her thoughts drift to Jacob Hill—to that first moment when he'd stepped onto that elevator and stolen her breath, to the way he kissed her, to how he'd looked at her after he'd done so.

Silly as it seemed, in that beat of time, she'd lost a little part of herself to him. And whether he admitted it or not, he'd lost a little piece of himself to her, too. She'd seen it in his eyes.

And it hadn't been just that. He'd gotten hard. She'd felt him when he'd pressed up against her, and remembering, alone in the tub, her body heated, tingled.

The carefully placed jets didn't help ease any of that but only heightened the arousal, leaving her aching and unfulfilled and…hungry for far more than a kiss, damn it.

She could imagine it, the two of them in bed. Given the way the man walked, talked and cooked with such utter confidence and effortless ease, she knew he would do things to her that would be out of this world.

"Ridiculous," she muttered, ruthlessly draining the tub before she could relive dessert, before she could picture how he'd looked at her as he'd fed her, how his eyes had flared when she'd licked her lips.

She was here to get him on the show! No more sex on the brain!

She had to figure out how to reach him, how to prove that her show would be different from whatever he was thinking it would be. Drying off, she climbed into the glorious bed, sliding against the silk sheets and thick comforter, her body still humming with lingering pleasure from the bath. It took a long time before sleep finally claimed her.

The next morning, after a night of Jacob-filled dreams, she sat up and laughed at herself. "No more," she said out loud. He was her job's salvation, which was far more important than a quick toss in the sack. Repeating it to herself like a mantra, she got dressed and called Liza.

"'Lo," came a very grumpy, sleepy voice.

"I need caffeine," Em said. "You with me?"

"I need someone to turn off the jackhammer inside my head," Liza groaned.

"Meet me downstairs. I have the next best thing."

"What's that, a lobotomy?"

"Aspirin."

"So YOU DIDN'T TELL HIM you wanted him for the show." Liza shook her head at Em and downed the aspirin.

They sat in a corner of the lobby, watching the world go by on the other side of the hotel windows, where pedestrians and cars whipped busily past them with the rushed sense of urgency characteristic of Manhattan.

"I tried to bring it up," Em said. "But he wasn't interested."

But Nathan was plenty interested, as proved by the ring of her cell phone. After looking at the ID, Em rolled her eyes at Liza, and answered.

"Sign the chef yet?" he asked.

"Working on it." She wondered if not mentioning that she was close only in her dreams was playing the "Hollywood game" the way he wanted her to.

Whether Nathan caught on, or if he was just worried, he paused. Then said, "Remember, Em. Do whatever you have to do to get him. Hell, use your feminine wiles."

Em looked at Liza in disbelief as she shook her head. "You did not just say use my feminine wiles."

"Why not? By all accounts, he's not bad to look at. You're single. Sleeping with him wouldn't be a hardship."

No, sleeping with Jacob wouldn't be a hardship. Too bad she'd be doing it for reasons entirely separate from the show. "Goodbye, Nathan."

"You're thinking about it," he said.

She growled.

He laughed. "Seriously, stay tough. Remember the hair-in-the-food trick."

Em hung up on him. She sighed and looked at Liza. "Here's the problem."

"You mean besides Nathan being a complete ass?"

"Yeah. I don't think Jacob's all that interested in his career at all, other than he enjoys what he does."

"Wait a minute." Liza narrowed her eyes. "Since when are you on a first-name basis with the chef?"

"Since that's his name."

Liza let it go, which meant her head still hurt, because it was unlike her to let anything go. "Are you *sure* he's not interested?"

Interested in the show? Or Em herself? "He runs the show here. He likes that. I don't see him happily letting a show run him."

Liza carefully rubbed her temples, her beauty looking a little strained this morning. "This aspirin needs to hurry up and kick in. Look, Em, just put it out there on the table for him, see what happens."

"I know."

"Today."

"I will. Eric," she said in surprise when he walked by.

He stopped, then with his eyes locked on Liza, came up to them. "Hey."

"What's up?" Em asked. "Want to have a seat? We're coming up with my plan of attack for approaching Jacob."

"I know an approach," Liza said as Eric sat. "Offer to have a wild fling with him. He wouldn't turn you down. No man who finds a woman attractive would turn her down." After having carefully avoided looking at Eric, she purposely turned her head to him. "Right, Eric?"

He cleared his throat. "Maybe he'd have his reasons."

"What reason could possibly be more important than making that woman feel good?" Liza pressed. "Than helping her out in her time of need?"

He glared at her. "Look, I didn't turn you down to insult you."

Liza snorted.

"Okay." Em stood up. "I'm going to leave you two alone—"

"Don't go," Liza said, snagging Em's wrist without taking her eyes off Eric.

"All I'm saying is that there *are* reasons," Eric said to Liza.

"Name one."

Em tried to pull free.

"I said don't go!" Liza snapped.

"Okay, that's it." Em gently but firmly extricated herself. "You two need to work this out, preferably by yourselves, without killing each other. Personally, I think you should work it out upstairs, maybe even in bed…."

Eric made some sort of strangled sound.

Liza just lifted a shoulder. "Can't. Eric has an aversion to getting in my bed these days."

Em put a hand on her friend's tense shoulder. "Stop torturing him."

"Tell him the same thing."

Eric shook his head.

Em kissed his cheek, then Liza's. "Be kind," she whispered to Liza, and walked off.

Caffeine, she decided. Now. A few other people were moving around, sitting on the black sofas talking, taking in the incredible artwork on display. She stopped in front of a large painting near the elevators, done in the bold strokes and colors of an early art deco piece. It was of a woman, nude, her hands outstretched, a look of ecstasy on her face as a man and another woman, also nude, attended to her. From their positions, one could assume the man took pleasure at a breast, the woman between her legs.

It should have been lewd, should have made the heat rise to Em's face, but instead she couldn't tear her eyes off the thing, not off the bright colors, or the boldly painted, beautiful bodies. In fact, she found herself just standing there, surrounded by the tranquility around her, absorbing it, breathing it in, trying to find her own center, her own sense of self, which was all tied into her job, into getting Chef Jacob Hill. She had to do this. "*I have to do this.*"

"Really?" It was the same low, husky voice as last night.

Jacob had come up to her side to look at the picture, too. "Which woman did you want to be?"

Just his proximity made everything within her react, tighten in anticipation, leap to attention. A little shocked at the effect he had on her, she turned her head and looked into his caramel eyes.

Yum, thought her body.

Watch out, thought her remaining working brain cells, and there weren't many.

He looked great, more than great, more like gorgeous in his work trousers, wool and gray and fitted to that long hard body, and a black dress shirt. His short, short hair seemed glossy beneath the lights. The scent of him alone should have been bottled and marketed as an aphrodisiac.

He arched a brow, waiting for an answer to his question, amusement swimming in his gaze. That look released something inside her.

She thought maybe it was the last of her resistance. "I didn't mean…" Damn it, she felt herself blush as she gestured to the painting. "I didn't mean I have to do *that*."

"No?" Tipping his head back, he looked at the two women in the picture again. "Now that's just a damn shame."

5

JACOB WATCHED EM SHIFT her weight from foot to foot
as she glanced again at the bold art deco painting of the
threesome. It made him want to smile. God, he loved to
ruffle her feathers.

"I really was talking about something else," she said.

"Like I said, it's really too bad."

Embarrassed or not, she met his gaze straight on. "So
it's true. Men really do fantasize about two women in
their bed."

"Doesn't have to be in bed." She rolled her eyes, and
he laughed. "You asked."

"I thought it was a myth. That men couldn't really
be so...so base."

"'Fraid not, and that we are."

She cocked her head and studied him thoughtfully.

"What's the draw? Two women? Seems like a lot of work."

"You mean 'cause there are two of every body part, and in some cases, four? Not work." He grinned.

"Women don't fantasize about two men."

"Never?"

She squirmed just a little, went a touch red, and he knew she was torn between lying or admitting a truth she preferred not to.

A minute ago he'd turned in the staff schedules for the week, and had planned on spending the next few hours on his own before he had to get started in the kitchen, but he'd seen her standing here and had been drawn to her like a metal rod to a magnet.

What was it about her? He wished he knew. He'd always been attracted to beautiful women, the more out-spoken and unabashedly sexual the better. Em was beau-tiful, no doubt, but neither outspoken nor unabashedly sexual, and yet she fascinated him. She stood there in a long floral skirt and cream angora sweater with a row of tiny buttons down the front, looking very together despite her blush and wry smile. She'd made an attempt at taming her hair, which amused him. The sides were pulled up in clips, but her long bangs had escaped, framing her jaw on either side. She wore gloss on her lips, something peachy, and he was hungry for it, for her.

Then there was the way she was looking at him, with a repressed yearning that stopped his jaded heart. Damn, her eyes were intoxicating, and suddenly, or maybe not so suddenly at all, he wanted to know what made her tick, what her bare skin felt like, what it tasted like, every inch of it. He wanted to see her lost in him, coming for him, wanted to feel her wrapped around him, panting his name.

No, make that *screaming* his name.

Em turned back to the erotically charged painting, but he put his hands on her arms and pulled her around to face him. Her eyes were a little dilated now, the pulse at the base of her throat racing. She was every bit as turned-on as he was, which made his condition worse. "Let's go."

"What? Where?"

He looked into her wary, but undoubtedly excited, eyes. "You up for an adventure, Emmaline Harris?"

"An adventure? I don't know…"

"Say yes."

She stared at him for a long moment. "Yes," she said softly, then hemmed when he led her to the front doors of the hotel. "Where are we going?"

"It's an amazing day out there, have you seen it?"

"I haven't been out yet."

"Can't stay inside all day. Not on a day like today." Jacob nodded to the doorman. It was Jon, who grinned and gave Jacob the thumbs-up sign behind Em's back.

As they stepped through the doors, a gust of wind wrapped around them in a chilly caress, and Jacob took a moment to admire how it molded Em's clothes to her belly, hips, legs and breasts, which were not big but not small, either, just right.

Unaware of his perusal of her body, Em tugged a rioting

strand of hair out of her mouth. "Jacob, there's something I really wanted to talk to you about first. My work—"

"No work. Not yet. Look at that sky." It was a brilliant, shimmering blue, and when Em tipped her head up, it brought a slow, beautiful smile to her face.

He stroked another wayward strand of hair from her cheek just for the excuse of touching her. "Come on. It's too perfect a day to waste." Taking her hand in his, he began walking.

Keeping up with him, she said, "Do you ever ask?"

"What?"

She shook her head. "I don't think you do. You just do whatever you want."

"Is that a problem?"

"I just can't believe women let you get away with it. Why would they? Wait, don't answer that." She looked baffled and just a little off her axis at the same time. "You are a very spoiled man, Jacob Hill."

"Spoiled?"

At that, she actually laughed at him at that, a sound he thoroughly enjoyed.

"I'm sorry," he said.

"You are not."

That tugged a grin out of him. "How about some coffee?" He spread his hands. "Hear that? I'm asking."

"You're teasing me is what you're doing. But yes. Coffee would be great."

He loved that, quiet or not, she spoke her mind. No pretense. No games.

Traffic was a bitch this morning, nothing new, so he

steered her through a throng of pedestrians, easily weaving her across the street between bikes and cabs and honking cars.

"Oh, my God," Em grumbled beneath her breath when a car came close. *"Crazy."*

"It's New York."

"In L.A.," she gasped breathlessly, as she kept up, "cars actually stop for people."

"Here, cars use pedestrians for parking spaces." He grabbed her arm and tugged her to him when a cab nearly did just that with her toes. "Stick close."

"Yikes," she muttered, but stayed against him. Now the strands of her hair stroked his face, the scent delicious enough that he wanted to breathe her in. As her long legs moved in tandem with his, he enjoyed the feel of her thigh brushing against his every step they took. Her breast was pressed up against his ribs and he wanted to turn her to face him, to savor the full experience, but when traffic slowed, she pulled away.

Where was a speeding cab when he needed one?

They walked through the gorgeous Bryant Park, an oasis in the midst of chaos, and were only one block from their destination when a bicyclist came out of nowhere, barreling down the middle of the sidewalk, without any apparent concern that they were in his way.

Perfect. Jacob turned toward Em, put his hands on her waist and pushed her back against the wall of the building at their right.

The bicyclist sped past, swearing at them for good measure.

Em lifted her head, blew a strand of hair out of her mouth and blinked at him. "That man should get a ticket."

"Not likely, not here." He touched her chilly cheek, letting his finger linger on her soft skin. "Em."

Her eyes flickered with something far more than irritation at the cyclist as she licked her lips and slowly raised her gaze to his. The pulse at the base of her neck beat like a poor overworked hummingbird's wings.

"I'm not going to ask if you mind this time," he said softly.

Understanding lit her gaze as he lowered his mouth toward hers. In spite of his words, he gave her the chance to stop him. Even a slight pressure from the hands she'd set on his chest would have done it. Instead she did the opposite, slowly curling her fingers into his shirt.

He smiled then, and as he kissed her, he thought, *That's the first time I've wanted to smile and kiss a woman at the same time.*

LOGICALLY EM KNEW this was a mistake but once Jacob's mouth touched hers, logic flew right out the window, and her body cut off all circulation to her brain cells, including the one that was supposed to say, "Don't even think about it!"

With a low, rough murmur deep in his throat, his hands came up and framed her face, sliding into her hair to palm her head, changing the angle of the kiss, deepening it.

Oh. My. God.

Helpless against the onslaught of pure lust, Em did as any woman who'd already tasted heaven and wanted to savor it some more would have done—she pulled him even closer and held on for all she was worth. But it was more than just his kiss, his touch. He aroused her physically, no doubt, and yet her need for him came from her heart, too.

If she could think, she'd have been terrified. But she couldn't think, couldn't do anything other than feel.

When his tongue slid to find hers, she heard a throaty, desperate sort of growl and realized it came from her.

Oh, boy. She was a goner.

It wasn't her fault, though. The man was the best kisser she'd ever been with. The best kisser on the planet. She shouldn't have been surprised. He was a walking dream.

And she didn't want to wake up.

So she tuned out the sounds of the streets around them—the talking, the footsteps, the honking of impatient drivers—and did what she knew she didn't do enough: let the experience wash over her. And it did wash over her, everything, his scent, deliciously male, the feel of his long, hard-muscled body pressed to hers, her soft thighs spread by one of his, and his hands…the way they slowly, knowingly glided up and down her arms, then up her throat to hold her face. It all simply undid her.

Finally, when he'd thoroughly ravished her with the kiss, he raised his mouth a fraction and opened his eyes, filled with a searing heat and desire and that ever-present wry amusement.

"What could possibly be funny?" she demanded, her knees still shaking.

"It's just that you kiss like you think."

She blinked. "I *what?*"

Again, that fleeting smile, the one that flashed his dimple and crinkled his drown-in-me eyes. "You, Emmaline Harris, are a series of contradictions. You dress like a businesswoman, for instance."

"I *am* a businesswoman."

"But you have a very carefree, come-what-may streak. It's sexy as hell, you know." He ran his thumb, rough with work calluses, over her lower lip, which was still wet from his mouth. She had to stifle the urge to suck the pad of it into her mouth.

What was happening to her? She'd always managed to go for stretches of time without thinking about sex. Or having sex. She'd slept with her last boyfriend—what had it been?—only four months or so ago. Not so long. Surely not long enough for this overwhelming longing, this heartbreaking ache to be sweeping through her body at the mere touch of his mouth or thumb.

"I see," she said, but she didn't. She had no idea where he was going with this, or where she wanted him to go with this, and yet when he spread his fingers over her jaw, she turned her face into his palm, pressing her lips there.

"I'm not sure what it is about you," he murmured, his voice a little husky now. "You talk like a schoolteacher. A little uptight, a little reserved."

Uptight? Reserved? She lifted her face away from his touch to look at him.

He smiled. "And yet you think things, things that have your eyes smoldering, things that bring heat to your face. Things that make me hot, Em."

She stared at him, no longer sure what she was feeling, though it caused her tummy to quiver and an embarrassing dampness to gather between her thighs.

"A contradiction," he whispered in that Southern honey of a voice that, along with his knowing smile, made her think of Matthew McConaughey in *How to Lose a Guy in 10 Days*. "Still up for caffeine?"

"Please."

He took her hand. As they began walking again, his long-legged easy stride eating up the sidewalk, she risked a quick sideways glance at him. *What was she doing?* She needed to get across the fact that she wanted him to host her TV show, and yet all she'd done so far was stare at him dreamily.

And kiss him. *Let's not forget that. Sheesh. Good going.*

"Here we are," he said, and stopped in front of a small hole-in-the-wall Irish pub called Patrick's.

Em stared at the Celtic sign swinging from the eaves. "But…it's ten in the morning."

"Yep." He opened the door for her.

She stepped inside, and was surprised. Even at this hour, the pub was filled, and with the mahogany bar and raw-wood floors and ceiling, the place felt warm and welcoming, exuding a natural charm. The conversation that greeted them was a good-natured mixture of gossip, wit and discussion. She could imagine sitting here comfortably with a drink, and when she looked at Jacob, could also imagine him perfectly at home in the middle of a brawl right there on the floor.

As if he'd read her mind, he grinned. "I've been known to escape here now and then."

"Isn't there a bar right in the hotel? Erotique, right?"

"Yes, but I feel more at home here." He pulled her up to the bar.

A woman came out of the back, sixtyish, with hair the color of a bright red crayon piled high on top of her head. She wore jeans and a T-shirt, with an apron that read, If Your Order Hasn't Arrived Yet, It's Probably Not Coming.

"Jacob, my love," she said with a heavy Irish accent and a surprised wide smile. "You came to cook up me day's special again!"

"That was for your birthday, Maddie."

"Damn." She sighed mightily. "I had a real hankering for one of your omelets…" Only someone with great love for someone else could lay on the guilt so thick.

Jacob looked at Em. "Em, meet Maddie. She owns this place and runs it with an iron fist, so watch out."

Maddie tossed back her head and laughed. "I'll iron fist you, boy. And don't think I can't." She hugged him hard, her head barely coming up to his chest. Then she pulled back and smacked his chest. "Now how about that special?"

Arm still around Maddie, Jacob looked at Em.

"I don't mind," she said, curious at the obvious great affection between the two of them.

"See, the girl doesn't mind." Maddie smiled innocently. "And then there's the added bonus of letting her see your soft side." She laughed again, and so did Jacob, as if they both found the possibility of Jacob having a soft side extremely funny.

"Come on, then," Jacob murmured to Em, leading her behind the bar, to the back. "Since you've let her get her way, there'll be no living with her."

Making himself right at home in the postage-stamp-size kitchen that had to be poorly equipped compared to what he was used to, he grabbed a pan and set it on the stovetop. Then he opened the refrigerator and said, "Heads up."

Em barely caught the red pepper he tossed her, and then the green one. And an onion— *"Hey."*

He straightened, his hands full with a carton of eggs and a hunk of cheese. Before her eyes, he chopped and diced and mixed it all up, hands moving quickly and efficiently, like a well-honed machine. God, was there anything sexier than watching a man in the kitchen? He caught her looking, and flashed her a dimple and a wink as he tossed the ingredients into the sizzling pan. And in less than two minutes, he was flipping an omelet in the air and then back into the pan.

Em couldn't tear her eyes off him. He wasn't just regular sexy, but beg-him-to-take-her sexy.

Maddie came into the kitchen in time for Jacob to hand her a loaded plate. Her carrottop hair wobbled as she leaned over the plate and took a bite, then grinned broadly. "Jacob, me boy, you've outdone yourself. I don't suppose you're going to do the dishes?"

Jacob laughed and led Em back to the front to her bar stool.

Maddie followed them out, still chewing. "Well, hell. I suppose I have to serve you now."

"We'll have two coffees," Jacob said. "Unless I need to brew that, too?"

"Smart-ass." Maddie moved back into the kitchen.

Jacob looked over at Em, his eyes full of laughter and mischief and memories of their kisses, maybe? Just thinking about them made the heat rush to her face, and to other parts of her body. "Jacob."

"Em," he said with mock obedience.

"I, uh, might have given you the wrong idea back there."

"Back there..."

"Outside."

He just looked at her.

Damn it. "When we kissed."

"Ah." He nodded seriously. "And what idea would that have been?"

"That I intend to sleep with you."

He arched a brow. "And you don't."

"No. I'm sorry." *No matter that you've made me so hot my skin is steaming.* "I don't."

Maddie came back with two mugs of coffee. Jacob didn't say anything while Em doctored hers up with sugar, lots of it, and cream. Not sure what to say, or how to get back to broaching the subject of her TV show, Em looked around her. The place had mismatched chairs and flooring that had probably been there for fifty years, yet was scrubbed to a shiny clean, as were all the surfaces. The crowd was much older than Hush's, and most were eating, not drinking. Two men past retirement age were playing cards in the corner. Others hunched at the counter over their mugs, some talking, some not. All the while Maddie ran the show with her boisterous voice and easy laughter. It was curious to Em that Jacob came here.

"Taste your coffee," he said with that uncanny way he had of reading her mind. "It'll make better sense to you."

She looked into Jacob's eyes, which matched the color of her coffee, thinking it'd be nice if he would read the rest of her mind, at least regarding the hosting gig. She took a sip of her drink, and the brew melted a delicious path all the way to her belly. "Oh. *Perfect*."

"Yeah." He smiled.

"No, I mean it. This is almost better than your food."

"Careful."

She laughed. "You been coming here a long time?"

"Oh, yeah." He looked at Maddie. "A long time."

It occurred to her how much she wanted to know him. Not the chef, but Jacob Hill, the man. "Tell me," she said quietly.

"The first time I showed up here, it was raining. Pouring, actually. It seemed like the skies had just opened up. I was cold and wet and hungry and, quite frankly, lost." His mouth twisted wryly. "At night, that hanging sign out front flashes like a beacon. Maddie harassed and badgered me, but she finally let me in."

"Why wouldn't she have?"

"I was fourteen."

Em gasped. "Fourteen? What was a fourteen-year-old doing alone on the streets of New York?"

"Ah." He sipped his coffee.

"Ah? What does that mean?"

"You probably had a curfew at fourteen."

"Well, of course I had a curfew at fourteen."

"And a bunch of rules."

"Yes."

"And you followed them."

"Well, not *always*." But mostly. Her parents had been wonderfully warm and loving, and yet even she had done her share of chafing at the teenage bit.

"Which means what?" he said. "That maybe you didn't always do your homework, or once you stayed out an extra five minutes?"

"I was basically a good kid," she admitted. "Big surprise, huh?" Their worlds couldn't have been more different, and yet those differences fascinated her. "Kids need boundaries. Where were your parents?"

"Never really had any."

Em couldn't even imagine, and her heart squeezed.

"Typical story," he said. "Young girl grows up in a trailer park outside of Nashville, dreams of getting out, gets herself knocked up by the first sweet-talker, who then vanishes at the special news. The unwanted baby grows up to be a kid who looks just like his daddy and the girl can't handle it."

He spoke easily enough, but Em's throat tightened at all he didn't say about those young, impressionable years when he'd thought of himself as the "unwanted baby." "What did you do?"

"Oh, I had a thing for cooking, even back then, and

a wanderlust spirit that made the whole thing an adventure. I left when I was ten. Never went back."

"Ten. My God, you were just a kid," she breathed, unable to even fathom it. "On your own like that...no one should be alone that young." She could hear the angry tears in her voice. "You should have been taken in by—"

"Social services? Hell, no." He let out a harsh laugh. "Happened once. It didn't work so well for me." Reaching out, he ran a finger over her temple, pushing her bangs from her eyes. "You have such beautiful hair."

She caught his hand. "We were talking about you."

"Then get that pity out of your pretty eyes. So I was young, it's no big deal."

"I'm not feeling pity," she said around the ball of emotion still lodged in her throat. "It's empathy. Anger for that kid you once were. How did you survive?"

"By cooking for traveling fairs across the South. I was pretty good. I did all right."

Having tasted his talents firsthand, she nodded. "Yes, you're extremely talented in the kitchen."

He shot her a wicked look. "Actually, I'm extremely talented in a number of areas."

Her stomach did a flip. "Finish your story." She'd intended a dry tone, but sounded more like Marilyn Monroe on a particularly hot summer day.

He touched her nose, looking amused. He knew what he did to her, and he liked it. "From the fairs, I progressed to hole-in-the-wall diners. Then I caught a train and ended up here in New York for a while. It's where I met Maddie. Her uncle took me in for a year—he worked at a culinary school uptown. I learned a bunch there but didn't have much loyalty in me then. I didn't stay."

"Where did you go?"

"Everywhere. I'd worked my way up to restaurants by that time." Shoving up the long sleeves of his black shirt, revealing corded forearms that made her mouth water, he picked up a set of knife, fork and spoon, and began to juggle them.

She just stared at him. She would have been no more surprised if he'd grown a set of horns.

"I was a real hit at the Japanese places, where they toss the ingredients and knives for the customers." Much to her disbelief, he added a plastic jam packet to the juggling items, leaning back a bit, craning his head up to keep everything in sight.

Maddie whooped her encouragement. The two old men in the corner stopped playing cards to watch.

All the other customers did the same.

Jacob grinned, then added yet another knife, a sharp one this time, his finely tuned body working effortlessly.

Em put a hand to her pounding heart.

"Don't worry," Jacob said. "I hardly ever miss and lose a finger."

Maddie wrapped her hands around her mouth. "Show-off," she yelled.

Jacob just kept up the amazing feat, his arms and hands moving so fast they were a whirl, his eyes carefully trained on the task as he continued his story. "Now I'm in the posh Amuse Bouche, happy to be there, of course, but…" With a grin, he leaned forward and planted a quick, hard kiss on Em's lips, all without dropping a single thing.

She could only stare at him.

He merely winked. "But I'm not nearly as sophisticated as people think."

Mouth dry, body not, Em could believe it.

6

JACOB WALKED EM BACK to the hotel, and though he realized she couldn't possibly know it, they walked right past his own building, where he kept an apartment.

He'd have loved to take her up there, show her his place. And his bed.

And his shower.

And his table.

And anywhere else where he could stretch out her willowy, warm body and take her.

This yearning for a beautiful woman wasn't new to him. But despite the long, hot, deeply sensual kisses they'd shared, and all they'd implied, she'd held herself back, leaving him aching for more.

And that *was* new.

When was the last time he'd had to work at getting a woman naked and mewling his name? He couldn't even remember. He just hoped she was worth the wait.

They were just outside the hotel when the phone at his hip vibrated, signaling an incoming text message from Pru.

Ended up going out last night, met the perfect woman for you. She's "the one," I swear it this time.

Delete.

JON OPENED THE DOORS for them with a professional, friendly smile for Em and another wink for Jacob.

They stepped into the stunning lobby and Em sighed. "It's so lovely in here. Warm and quiet, yet…exciting."

Jacob liked the exciting part, and might have pursued the comment but his cell phone vibrated to life again.

Stop deleting me. Pru.

With great satisfaction, he hit Delete again.

"Problem?" Em asked.

"Remember the two women from the elevator yesterday?"

"Your friends?"

"Soon to be ex-friends? One of them is at it again."

"Tell her you're otherwise occupied."

"Am I?"

That put an extremely kissable look on her face but before he could lean in, his phone went off yet again. "Excuse me," he said grimly, and, ignoring the incoming message, entered one of his own.

Pru, goddamn it, tell Caya how you feel about her instead of bugging the shit out of me. In fact, you tell her, or I will.

There. That ought to do it. He waited a moment, but his phone remained still and blessedly silent. With satisfaction, he shoved it deep into his pocket. "Where were we?"

"Well…"

"Ah, I remember. You were going to tell me if I'm otherwise occupied."

She stared at him, with those mossy-green eyes. "You're teasing me."

"Yeah." Even though it was time for him to be getting into the kitchen to begin preparing, he walked her through the lobby toward the elevators, where he pushed the button for the twelfth floor.

"I can get myself back to my room," she said, clasping her hands together. "Really. But thanks."

He eyed her with amusement. "Are you afraid to get on the elevator with me, Em?"

She tilted her chin up. Her bangs were stabbing into her eyes, and she'd long ago nibbled off any lip gloss. A shame because he'd have liked to have nibbled it off himself.

"Don't be silly," she said.

When he just looked at her, she caved. "Not afraid. Let's call it…off balance, and you don't have to look so pleased," she said, putting a finger to his chest. "Or smug."

He couldn't stop his smile from spreading, which in turn had her letting out a rough laugh herself. "It's just that I'm not used to the way you leave me deaf, dumb and blind every time you kiss me, if you must know."

The doors opened and he gently nudged her inside, following close behind.

She eyed him with an arousing mix of wariness and

excitement. The doors closed and he stepped toward her, closing in on her space.

She backed up.

His phone vibrated at his hip. He didn't even glance at it. Another step had her against the mirror.

She looked down her nose at him. "Intimidation?"

"Nope." He had no idea who was really seducing whom when he hauled her up on her toes and kissed her softly. "Just helping you get used to me leaving you deaf, dumb and blind." And then he kissed her again.

Not so softly.

THE MOMENT HIS MOUTH touched hers, Em knew she was in trouble. She'd begun to know him now. She admired what he'd done with his life, and she liked the man he'd become. Those things, combined with the sensual hold he had on her—figuratively as well as literally—made him damn irresistible, as evidenced by her low sigh of acquiescence.

At the sound, Jacob slid his hands into her hair to hold her head as he plundered. He'd been right, it was another deafening, muting, blinding kiss, but she wasn't going down easily. She tore her mouth free and gasped, "I don't think—"

"Perfect. Stick with that." He came at her again, cutting off any other words she might have come up with, weak excuses for why they shouldn't, why they couldn't, and she might have managed an excuse or two if she hadn't been drowning in pure, unadulterated lust.

This was a taking kiss, an I'm-the-man sort of kiss

that might have pissed her off if it had been anyone other than Jacob Hill. She was so aroused she could hardly stand. No matter, he had her pressed back against the wall, holding her up with his delicious, hard body, and if that hadn't been enough, he had his tongue deep in her mouth with a hungry, urgent stroke that took her breath away.

When air was required by them both, he lifted his head and stared at her. The elevator rolled to a stop, and, without breaking eye contact, he reached out and slapped a hand over the close-door button.

His eyes beamed with intent. "Where were we?"

Oh, my. "Um…"

"Never mind. I've got it." And still holding the button down, he again lowered his head.

With the cold, hard mirrors at her back and the warm, hard man at her front, she hesitated for one beat of her poor, overexcited heart, and then sank into the kiss.

He murmured his pleasure, deepening the kiss. She met him halfway, sinking her fingers into the defined muscle of his shoulders and holding on for dear life.

"God, you taste sweet," he murmured, shifting his mouth to nibble at the corner of hers, then her jaw, making his way to her ear, while his free hand stroked languidly up and down her back, squeezing her hip, then lower, palming her bottom.

When his fingers danced down and touched bare skin, she jumped, realizing he'd skimmed the hem of her skirt up so that he could caress the backs of her thighs.

And then between them.

"So sweet," he murmured again, spreading hot, open-mouthed kisses down her throat, nudging her sweater aside as he traced her collarbone with his tongue.

Panting, her head thunked back against the mirror, determination and all thoughts of her show gone. "Jacob."

"Yeah, right here." With his hands occupied, one still on the close-door button, the other beneath her skirt, he couldn't open her sweater, so he merely worked his way around that by sucking it into his mouth along with her breast.

She felt his tongue, hot and wet through the thin layer, and gasped. Then gasped again when he gently sank his teeth into her. And yet again when he pressed a finger against her, slowly tracing the edge of her panties.

Oh, God, she thought in a sudden panic, *am I wearing granny panties? Do I even care?* It shocked her how much she wanted to let go, how much she wanted to slap her own hand over the close-door button to free up his, so that he could put *both* hands on her body and take her, take her now, here, in an elevator, a semipublic place, where they could be seen, where maybe there were even cameras…

"Stop."

He went still, then slowly lifted his head, blinking those sleepy, sexy-lidded eyes at her.

"We can't," she said. "Not here."

He blew out a careful breath, looking hot, and just a little bothered.

"There are probably cameras…" Feeling silly, she trailed off. After stepping clear, she smoothed down her clothes, staring ridiculously primly at the closed doors, which slowly began to open. She exited quickly, then whirled back to face him, only he'd followed her off and she plowed right into him. "It's just that I never got to tell you. And you…"

"What?" he asked, his hands coming up to her arms.

God, it would sound so wrong now. She'd waited too long. Whirling again, she headed toward her room, fumbling through her purse to find her room card. He took it from her fingers and opened her door, waiting for her to go inside before following her.

The beachy elegance of the room cut through some of her tension, which came back full force when she caught sight of her reflection in the wide seashell mirror over the dresser.

Her hair, wavy on the best of days, had rioted, curling around her flushed face. Her eyes seemed huge and misty, dreamy, and her lips—still wet from his kiss— were full and puffy. Her sweater had a wet spot over one breast, and her nipples pressed against the material. She looked as though she'd just been thoroughly ravaged, which of course she had.

Jacob came up behind her and ran his hands up her arms. "Look at you."

She was looking. She couldn't look away. She blinked, but the same image presented back to her: one Emmaline Harris, rumpled and tousled, and smiling. No, that wasn't right. No smiling. Not until she told him. She swiped the ridiculous grin from her face. "Jacob."

"Uh-huh." His mouth was skimming her neck again,

and the reflection of his dark head bent to her, eyes closed. Those long dark lashes against his cheeks, his tongue touching her flesh, made her shiver.

"Jacob," she said again, stronger this time, and turned to face him.

But Jacob Hill in the flesh was even more compelling than his mirror image had been. His eyes were very hot, and his mouth curved in a little knowing smile that said *I can make you come in less than three minutes*.

Given how close to that orgasm she actually felt, he could probably do it in three *seconds*. She took a big gulp of air.

His eyes cut to her bed, freshly made by housekeeping, with what appeared to be a small basket in the middle of the mattress.

With compliments from Sous-Chef Hill the note read, and she looked at him. "You sent this to me?"

"It's the makings for s'mores. You'll love them."

She had to laugh. "Do you ever doubt yourself?"

He frowned, thinking. "Sure."

"When?"

"Well…" He strode closer, tracing a finger along her hairline. "Now, for instance. Because somehow I know you aren't going to invite me onto that mattress with you."

"No." Her voice was far weaker than she would have liked. "No," she repeated. "I'm not. Jacob…" God, this was harder now that she'd touched him, kissed him. Now that she knew him. So much harder. "I've told you I'm a TV producer."

"Yes."

"What you don't know is that I have one month to get my show off the ground or I'm fired."

"Some reality show, right?"

"Yes." She'd never wanted to say anything less than what she had to say now. "A cooking show."

A little furrow appeared between his eyes as he digested her words. "As in a chef in front of a camera whipping up cookies kind of cooking show?"

"I was thinking something a little more interesting than that." Nerves fluttered in her belly. She'd wanted to recruit him, but now she just wanted him.

"Like what exactly?" His voice had cooled, the drawl thickened. He was irritated, with good reason.

"Well…"

"Should I guess, Em?" His eyes grew icy, too. "You heard about Amuse Bouche, and the success we've had."

"Actually, I heard about you."

"And you thought I'd, what? Drop everything and coming running to Hollywood to smile for a camera on some cable show? Did you really?"

"It's a prime-time show, on a major network." She offered him a weak smile, which faded when he just looked at her. "I'm doing this all wrong," she said quickly. "I meant to woo you, to make it sound really appealing and interesting, which it should be. It's TV, Jacob. A show of your own. Your input would be welcome, of course, and—"

"My input would be welcome," he repeated slowly, then shook his head. "Let me get this straight. You want me to go to Hollywood and cook in front of a camera like…like a caged animal."

She didn't know how to respond to that.

"Jesus," he breathed, backing up a step, shaking his head. "You're serious. You're completely serious."

"Jacob—"

"Wow." He prided himself on his street smarts, on his worldliness, on the fact that he was sharp enough never to be taken. But this sweet, beautiful woman had walked right through his defenses with one kiss.

He was saved from having to admit that by a knock on the room door.

"Em?" came a female voice. "Open up."

Em jumped, then whipped around and stared at herself in the mirror. "Oh, boy." She stroked a hand down her sweater and shot Jacob an indecipherable look. "That's Liza, my assistant, and also close friend." She looked good and flustered, and distractedly shoved at her bangs.

Jacob felt his body stir just looking at her, and had to back up another step. No. She'd pissed him off, so no more thinking about her that way.

"I know this is crazy," she whispered, putting her hands on his chest. "But please, give me a chance to explain everything to you."

No need. That first kiss in the elevator had been his own doing, an amusing coincidence he could see now, fate playing a joke on the both of them. But she'd had plenty of opportunities between then and now to explain her business here. That *he*, in fact, was her business here.

But she hadn't.

The thing was, he didn't blame her. He knew desperation, and he recognized it well, so the thing to do here, the only thing to do here, was cut his losses and get over it, and over her.

Liza knocked again, louder now. "Emmaline!"

"Give me a minute," Em called to the door.

"Why?" Liza demanded. "Are you having wild monkey sex in there with the hot stud-muffin chef?"

Jacob choked back a laugh.

Unbelievably, Em glared at him, as if this was *his* fault, and scrubbed a hand down her face.

"Em, come on, I'm standing out here in my slut outfit," Liza said urgently through the door. "I tried it on and I want you to see if it's good enough to drive Eric out of his mind with crazed jealousy. I'm going to drag him to Exhibit A tonight, the basement bar where there's nude dancing. People supposedly do it in the booths, can you believe it? Now I need you to take a look at me and make sure I'm not too over the top, so open up."

"Oh, my God—" Looking as if she'd hit the boiling point, Em broke off, moved to the door and hauled it open.

Liza stood there in a canary-yellow micromini, cut nearly up to her crotch. A matching crop top, do-me lipstick and go-go boots designed to stop brain cells in their tracks completed the look.

"Oh, my God," Em repeated, looking her friend and assistant up and down. "Did you look in the mirror after you put that horror on?"

Liza opened her mouth, but then at the sight of Em looking the way she did—as if she'd just had that "wild monkey sex" Liza had mentioned—she shut her mouth again. "I don't think the subject here should be my outfit," Liza finally said.

"It's not what you think," Em said.

"Really?" Liza moved into the room, nodded to Jacob and then looked back at Em. "Because what I'm thinking is that you just got thoroughly laid. So does this mean you're in?" she asked Jacob.

"In?"

"Are you going to do the show and save Em's ass, cute as it may be?"

Jacob looked at Em.

Em sighed. "We were in the early talks."

"Yes, well, talks are officially over." Jacob moved toward the door, where he made the mistake of brushing past Em. He stopped.

She tipped her head up and stared at him with regret and embarrassment, and lingering arousal. Lifting a finger, he stroked it over her jaw—God, he loved her skin. "'Bye, Em."

"Jacob—"

Nope. Never look back. A mantra he was particularly fond of. With a shake of his head, he walked out of her room, shutting the door behind him.

"Tell me everything," he heard Liza say.

"You'd better sit down," Em replied, which threw Jacob off his stride just a little.

She'd gotten to him. No doubt, she'd gotten to him.

7

To: Sous-Chef Jacob Hill
From: Concierge
Maddie from Patrick's just delivered a pot of
coffee here for you, on request of the guest in
room 1212. Odd, since as you know, we have our
own excellent blend right here at Hush. Call when
you come in. We'll deliver it to you.

JACOB STOOD IN THE LOBBY, in front of the concierge
desk, holding the memo that had been taped to his locker.

"I'd have brought the coffee to you," Deidre said.
One of four Hush concierges, Deidre was his personal
favorite. Not only could she get any answer anyone ever
needed, but with her bright pink hair, multiple piercings
and pixie face, she looked damn good while doing it.

The two of them had dated once.

Correction. They'd slept together once.

At the time, Deidre had felt the same way as Jacob,
more than one night constituted something far too
close to a relationship, and they'd happily gone their
separate ways.

Since then, Deidre had gone on to other things—meaning other men. But now she was looking at him again, with that once-familiar heat. "Busy tonight?" she asked, handing over Maddie's large thermos.

"I thought you were dating some purple-haired guy." There was another note taped to the thermos.

Deidre lifted a shoulder. "I've moved on."

He cut her a glance. "He got too serious, huh?"

"Damn men." She sighed. "They always do."

"Maybe you're just irresistible."

She grinned. "Don't you know it. So tonight…? There's a new band playing at Erotique. Want to meet me there for a few drinks?"

He was about to reply but he'd just scanned the note—from Em—and it sidetracked him.

Jacob,

I know, I know. Coffee as a forgiveness bribe—tacky. But please believe me, I never meant to keep my reason for being in NY a secret. It's just that you're quite different from anyone I've ever met, and, well, potent. Please let me make it up to you. However you'd like. There, I bet that got your attention. Come see me anytime, anywhere. I'll be at Hush all day. Enjoy Maddie's incomparable coffee, Jacob. Best, Em.

"Yoo-hoo, earth to Chef." Deidre waved a hand in his face. "Come in, Chef."

"Yeah." Jacob crumpled up the note. Deidre lifted her

small black trash can so he could toss the note in. But he held on to the paper, which, if he wasn't mistaken, actually smelled like Em.

When he looked back at Deidre, her smile slowly faded. "Wow."

"What?"

"That look on your face." She stared at him in disbelief. "Who's the gift sender?"

"It's just coffee."

"Yeah, but that's not just a smile on your face."

He did his best to swipe off the grin.

She slowly shook her head. "The remnants are still there."

He snatched up the thermos, shot her a long look and began to walk away.

"You can run," she called after him. "But you can't hide, not from me. I have a responsibility to the rest of the staff to spread the correct gossip about you. Talk to me! *Chef!*"

He lifted a hand and kept going.

"Damn it," he heard her mutter, and any other time he might have laughed, but he didn't feel like laughing.

He felt like… Hell, he had no idea what he felt like. Unused to the feeling, he walked through the lobby, past Erotique, thinking a drink would be a great thing— if it hadn't been so early.

He entered Amuse Bouche. Pru met him just outside the kitchen door, also unusually quiet and subdued as she balanced her briefcase and a box loaded with four bottles of different wines. "You're early, too," she said.

He took the box from her. "What's wrong with being early?"

"It's a rare phenomenon, that's all. In fact, you're usually late enough that someone has to page you out of some woman's bed to get your ass in here."

"Well, good day to you, too."

Eyes unhappy, she shrugged.

"What, don't have the phone number of that woman you want me to call?" he teased when she failed to continue with her usual pestering. "No blind dates for me?"

When she only sent him a halfhearted smile, he stopped. "What's the matter?"

"Nothing."

He looked at her closed, miserable face. "It's something."

She shrugged, and walked ahead of him into the kitchen, setting her briefcase down on the black granite counter and taking the box from him.

"Pru."

Another shrug. Woman-speak for *Drag it out of me, please*.

He again took the box and set it next to her briefcase. "Where did you and Caya end up last night?"

"Erotique. We met up with some of her friends from before."

Before was any time before Caya had come to live with Pru. Pru liked it when the world revolved around her.

"Then we went down to Exhibit A," she said.

Jacob arched a brow, signaling his surprise that Pru

would want to take Caya there, the place in Hush that was undoubtedly the most uninhibited, wild and adventurous. Possibly in all of Manhattan. "Did you tell her how you feel?"

"About what, that I don't like her wild friends? That I don't like how much she goes out? That I especially don't like the way she tries to lose her problems in casual sex?"

"No," Jacob said. "That you want her for yourself."

"Of course I didn't tell her that. It's going to ruin the friendship."

"No, it's not."

"This can't be happening to me," Pru said softly, pacing the room. "Love sucks, remember?"

"Hey, I didn't say anything about love."

"Oh, my God." Pru stopped and covered her face. "Oh, my God. I love her."

Shaken now, Jacob stared at her. "Okay, let's not get carried away."

"No, it's true. I love her." Stricken, Pru dropped her hands, then whirled on her heel.

"Where are you going?"

"To think. To obsess. To have my nails done before I chew them all to the quick."

"Pru—"

"Don't talk to me right now."

Suited him just fine. He didn't like talking anyway. What the hell was wrong with him, trying to help?

Or spending so much time thinking about Em when he had plenty of other women in his life to screw it up?

When he could no longer hear Pru's heels clicking angrily away, he leaned back against the counter and poured himself a mug of Maddie's finest from the thermos. Sipping the brew, he reread Em's note.

Twice.

When he caught himself reading it a fourth time, he crumpled it up again and tossed it in the trash. And reminded himself he never looked back, not ever.

EM, LIZA AND ERIC were having an emergency meeting. Because she'd screwed up. The thought made her wince, because it was true, she'd blown it. She'd lost herself in Jacob and had forgotten the goal. Now he felt used, and she couldn't blame him.

They were having the meeting by the pool, which was on the glass-covered roof. The area had scattered wrought-iron benches and freestanding fountains, and was warmed with tall gas-powered heaters designed like lanterns. All this was surrounded by lush greenery and wildly colorful blooms, despite the fact that in the real world, it was February in New York. The incredible beauty had a calming effect on Em's frazzled nerves. The pool itself was Olympic-size, with a large hot tub next to it, and a fully stocked bar for their drinking pleasure.

She lay on the cushiest white lounge chair she'd ever enjoyed, in a bathing suit. From here they were going to move their meeting into the spa. Liza had insisted, claiming they were far too busy back in Los Angeles for such foolishness, and that they should experience the full scope of what New York had to offer.

Especially now that it looked as if they were all headed toward the unemployment line.

Liza had booked them all for a variety of spa luxuries, a few of which Em had never even heard of. It seemed surreal, lying here, sunning as if they were lizards on a rock, being served their every wish by attentive, professional personnel.

While guilt and regret fought for space in her belly.

Liza had a drink in her hand, a pretty-colored something with an umbrella sticking out of it. Eric was face-down on his lounge and had a lovely attendant rubbing lotion onto his shoulders.

Every time he moaned his pleasure, Liza took a long sip of her drink.

Em leaned close to Liza. "You could just tell him he's getting to you," she whispered.

"Are you kidding?" she whispered back, adjusting her bikini top so that her breasts were plumped up and practically falling out. "Never give a guy the upper hand. Besides, I've got him just where I want him."

Em eyed Eric, who was still very much enjoying his massage. "If you say so."

"Oh, forget him," Liza said with a sniff, but she flipped over, revealing her thong bikini bottoms. Or more to the point, her extremely perfect yoga-tightened butt.

From Eric's chair came a choking sound. When they looked over at him, he turned his head away.

Liza sent Em a smile. "See? Right where I want him."

Em shook her head.

"So tell me again why we sent coffee to a man who

could probably get any coffee in the city that he wanted, especially from his own hotel?"

Em sat back against the cushy lounge chair and sighed. "Because I'm trying to apologize to him."

"Because why?"

"Because he deserves it. I should have told him sooner, Liza."

"Really? When, exactly? When he was kissing you in the elevator?"

"Yes, well, certainly by that second kiss."

Liza's eyes nearly bugged out of her head.

Even Eric sat up for this one.

"*Second kiss?*" they both asked together.

Em rolled her eyes. "Look, this isn't exactly the time to discuss how many kisses there were."

"When exactly would be a good time then?" Liza asked. "The next time I find you two having wild monkey sex in your room?"

"We were not having wild monkey sex," Em said with exaggerated patience.

"What about regular sex?" Eric asked hopefully. "Because you could tell us about that."

Liza shoved him back to his lounge. "Perv."

"I'm just saying she should get it off her chest," he said innocently. "That's all."

"There's nothing to get off my chest," Em assured the both of them. "And we're here to talk about the real issue, that being the chef for the show."

"Or the lack thereof," Liza pointed out.

"Yes, thank you, Liza. Or the lack thereof. A situation

that needs to be fixed, immediately. I'm going to find a way to talk to Jacob. I'm not giving up there, but…" Em's stomach clutched yet again. She felt funny opening her briefcase and pulling out a pad of paper in her bikini, but desperate times… "Any thoughts just in case?"

"Hire me," Eric said.

Liza laughed.

Eric turned his face toward the sun, his expression unreadable. "Well, if that's so funny, audition for other chefs." He sprawled facedown on his lounge again, stretching his long, lean body as he sunned. "Right here at Hush."

Liza and Em looked at each other in shocked surprise. "You know," Liza said, "once in a while he actually has a few productive thoughts."

"I've got a few more," Eric assured her with a naughty tone in his voice. "Want to hear them?"

"No," Liza said.

Eric shrugged and lay back down, facing away from them.

This left Liza free to openly study his slicked-up, smooth back and butt, with such an expression of longing it hurt to look at her.

"Tell him you want him," Em mouthed.

Pride blaring from her gaze, Liza shook her head.

Em sighed and began to make her list. "We'll need to book a conference room."

"And get the word of the auditions out," Liza added.

"I can do that." Eric mumbled this into his lounge pillow. "I've got agents I can call. Don't worry, I'll get you a decent showing."

It had to be done, Em thought as Eric and Liza continued to come up with good ideas. They had to have a viable backup if Jacob truly wasn't interested. She could do that, find someone else with the charisma and talent she needed. Because she couldn't lose sight of the real issue—this was her last chance. If she screwed this up, by this time next month she'd be standing behind a counter in a silly hat, asking customers if they wanted red or green sauce with their tacos.

"Excuse me," came a low, soothing female voice. "We're ready for you in the spa."

Eric and Liza jumped up eagerly. Em wrapped herself in one of Hush's thick towels and followed the woman through the gorgeous garden that someone worked very hard on. The moment they entered the spa, Em let out a deep, tense breath she hadn't even realized she'd been holding.

She could smell a myriad of special scents, mostly lavender, and the walls glowed with a gentle light that was nearly as soothing as the scent. In the reception area there was a wall of cascading water that both looked and sounded incredibly appealing. It was so beautiful in here it made her ache, and the quiet surrounded her, a calming balm on her shaky spirit.

They were each led into separate rooms. Em's had a freestanding waterfall similar to the one in her room. There was incense burning, and the soft sounds of a jungle coming from speakers she couldn't see. An attendant told her about an Indo-Asian hot oil treatment. "A delight to the senses," she promised in a soft, quiet voice that went with the atmosphere. "When you're ready, remove your suit, stretch out on the massage table and just concentrate on relaxing."

Braving the moment, Em stripped out of her bathing suit, covered herself with a sheet so soft it felt like a cloud and lay down. The attendant came back in and started the massage, using heated oil that had Em melting into the table. Her skin soaked up the oil, and by the time it was over, she didn't think she had a single bone left in her body.

Then she was wrapped in warm, herb-soaked strips of linen and covered with the sheet, left to bake pleasantly under a heat lamp. Once alone, she listened to the sounds of the water hitting the rocks, of the faraway jungle, and nearly forgot all about her troubles. In fact, her entire being began to let go for the first time in a very long time.

The door opened. "Look at that," someone said in a very low, husky Southern drawl. "Just what the doctor ordered—Emmaline Harris, bound and stretched out for my perusal."

Em, flat on her belly, trussed up in her herb-soaked linens and sheet like a mummy, barely lifted her head. It was all the movement she could manage.

Jacob's mouth was curved in a smile, but it wasn't necessarily a friendly one. It held things, naughty, wicked things, and made her tummy tremble.

"What are you doing here?" she asked, struggling to sit up.

He held up a piece of paper. Her note, written to him in her own hands, inviting him to please come see her today, anytime, anywhere.

Admittedly, not her smartest idea. An open invitation.

Interestingly enough, the note was crinkled, as if he'd balled it up, then smoothed it out.

And if she took a good look at him, she could see his jaw was tight enough to tic, that those broad shoulders seemed tightened as hard as rocks.

Chef was looking a little tense.

"Jacob," she said, still fighting the linen. "I'm so sorry I hurt your feelings."

"You didn't." He moved close, watching her tussle with the sheet for a moment before he gave her a hand, helping her to a sitting position so that her legs hung over the edge.

She kept a hold on the sheet wrapped around her body—her only armor—clutching it close, hoping not to expose any body parts. "I wanted to talk to you," she said, "about the show."

He hadn't backed up. His thighs bumped her knees. "I'm not here to talk about the show."

"Oh." She smoothed the sheet over her legs, feeling the strips of linen beneath beginning to loosen. "But—"

"No business in here." Reaching out, he stroked a finger over her shoulder—her bare shoulder—making her painfully aware that her sheet had slipped. With only the strips of the herb-soaked linen beneath, she wasn't completely bare, but she felt pretty damn naked all the same.

Jacob was just looking at her, his eyes dark and un-readable, leaving her feeling like Little Red Riding

Hood staring into the eyes of the hungry wolf. She fought with the sheet a minute, tugging, letting out a sound of vexation because it was trapped under her butt.

Jacob watched, a slight smile on his lips.

She finally managed to pull some of the sheet free from beneath her so that she could cover her shoulders, only she pulled too much.

And felt nothing but table beneath her.

Oops.

To complicate her situation—and this was most definitely a situation—her linen strips were loosening. Feeling extremely naked now, she squirmed about some more, trying to get herself completely covered, but it just wasn't happening. "Maybe you could give me a hand here…"

He just slid his hands into his pockets. "You're doing just fine."

Oh, yeah. If fine was giving him a show! With some fancy maneuvering, she got her bare butt covered again—

A sound escaped Jacob at the exact moment she realized she felt cool air brushing over a breast.

Oh, God. She'd created her own Nipplegate. She told herself he couldn't possibly be able to see in the dim room, and dared a quick peek at him.

His eyes were seriously smoldering. She heard the rough breath whoosh out of his lungs.

He'd seen.

"Damn it." Leaping off the table, she pulled the sheet tight around her and prepared to lie back down, but it was too late. Beneath her, the herb-soaked linen began to slide down her body, hitting the floor. *Plop. Plop. Plop.* "This is all your fault," she said.

He lifted his hands. "I'm not doing anything."

"You don't have to. That's the point."

"Except become a cooking show host."

She let out a breath and hugged the sheet closer. "Look, if you believe nothing else, believe that I'm sorry about that."

With characteristic bluntness, he let his gaze roam over her, from her out-of-control hair, to the sheet she was hugging around her for all she was worth, to her bare toes. Without a word, he again stepped closer, staring into her eyes while the pad of his finger stroked over the very base of her throat, at the pulse she knew was drumming there. An innocent enough touch, but it felt intimate. Forbidden. And she wanted more, a realization that made her swallow hard.

His gaze locked on the movement her throat made, and his finger trailed down, over her collarbone.

Her nipples hardened.

In reaction, he let out a very male sound and slowly ran a finger over her bare shoulder, leaving a line of tingly awareness she didn't know what to do about. She stood there without a stitch on except the sheet, painfully aware of herself and the picture she must make, completely naked while he was fully clothed and yet…yet so aroused her skin felt too tight.

His finger retraced its trail, everywhere he touched creating a path of fire. She sucked in a breath.

So did he. "Tell me what you feel," he said.

You, making me shaky with lust. You, taking me to a place I'm not ready for. "I don't—"

"Tell me."

"Heat." Her voice cracked so she cleared her throat and said it again. "I feel heat."

"It's the oil," he told her, his hand smoothing slowly up and down her back. "It's seasonally blended to create a warming effect in cool weather. It works the opposite way when it's hot outside."

"Oh." An embarrassed smile escaped her. "I thought—"

"What?"

"That it was you." Her eyes drifted shut. "Whenever you're touching me, I feel so…"

"Aware?"

"*Yes.*"

"That's the calamus root and sandalwood powder." His voice was low and quiet, and incredibly arousing, as much as the oil and his manipulation of it on her body. The man would be a huge asset to any spa, his presence alone making it millions of dollars.

"The combination is meant to stimulate." His gaze held hers as his finger kept moving over her, lower than her collarbone now, just barely skimming the upper curve of her breast, right at the edge of the sheet. "But I'm very much enjoying that you thought it was me making you feel so aware." His finger slipped just beneath the edging of the sheet.

"Jacob," she gasped.

He used the backs of his fingers now, his knuckles brushing over her.

She couldn't help it, she watched his fingers on her breast, mesmerized by the erotic sight of his big, tanned hand on her pale, creamy skin. Though her nipple was still covered by the sheet, barely, it poked against the material, begging for equal attention.

Other parts of her body were clamoring for attention, too.

He kept giving it, until she was a quivering, anticipatory wreck.

"I can't stand any more," she whispered. "*Please...*"

Putting his hands on her shoulders, he slowly turned her away from him.

She stood there wondering what he was going to do to her, the wondering made more all the overpowering because she could no longer see him.

"Onto the table," he murmured, wrapping his fingers in her sheet at the base of her spine.

"Hey." She grasped it between her breasts, held on to it for dear life. If she moved, the sheet would stay with him, falling away from her body.

She was *not* ready for that.

"Lie back down," he said softly from just behind her, his breath rustling the hair over her ear. "I'll cover you."

Unable to let go, she shook her head. "I can't."

"Go on," he said with a tone she hadn't heard from him before: tenderness.

Craning her head, she looked back at him. His eyes

flickered with a tenseness that matched hers, but in a blink it was gone.

"Lie back down," he said. "You don't want to waste all the relaxing you've done."

"Too late," she muttered.

With infinite patience, he waited her out.

Closing her eyes, she took a deep breath and then let go of the sheet.

He surprised her, holding the sheet up between them, blocking his view of her as she lay down. Then it fluttered over her, covering her from midback to midthigh, and she let out a breath, only to have it clog her throat when he stroked a hand down her back, reactivating the oil, heating her up in an instant.

She kept her eyes tightly closed, concentrating on what he made her feel, but unable to let go of the tenseness she'd seen in his expression when he'd first walked in. "Jacob?"

"Hmm?"

Over the sheet, his fingers moved on her lower back, pressing lightly in just the right spot to make her want to stretch and purr like a kitten. "Are you…okay?"

Ignoring her question, he moved up her spine and then back down again. "You smell like something a man might want to gobble up."

"You're changing the subject—" She broke off to moan when he got to her shoulders and dug in.

"Good?" he asked.

So good she'd beg if he stopped. "Please talk to me."

He sighed as his fingers made their way back down

her spine, slowly, with unbelievable talent. "You have a one-track mind."

And so, she was willing to bet, did he. "Talk."

He skimmed over her bottom, which had her clenching her cheeks, but he didn't stay and linger, not until he got to the backs of her thighs. While he worked there, another helpless moan fluttered out of her lips before she could stop herself.

"Why don't you just concentrate on the pleasure?" he asked. "Stop holding back."

"Not until you talk to me."

"You're not going to like it."

She already knew that. "Try me."

One finger traced a silky path up the back of her thigh to the very edge of the sheet, and then a little farther. "I can't stop thinking about you."

She tried to turn over so she could see him but he held her down with one big, warm hand at the middle of her spine. "No, don't move. Just stay on your stomach. I'll go. Your attendant will be back in a few."

"But…"

But nothing. Whether it had been her reaction, or that he felt he'd said too much, he was gone.

Letting her cheek touch the table again, she lay there, mind racing, body aching, heart pounding, pounding, pounding.

He couldn't stop thinking about her.

Well, that made them even.

8

To: Spa attendants
From: Spa manager
Re: Herbal wraps
New as of today! Stay in room once herbal wrap is applied to keep guest relaxed and immobile. Otherwise, the linens apparently may unravel and fall off.

"THEY'RE HOLDING open auditions here today for some new cooking show."

This was what Jacob heard the next day when he got to his kitchen. Pushing open the doors, he found Caya and two other servers gathered around, talking.

Caya grinned at him. "Did you hear?"

"Yeah," he managed to say without a grimace. "I've heard." Though due to his own stubbornness, he knew none of the details. He didn't want the details. He wanted things to go back to normal.

"Maybe I should try out," Caya said. "I could become famous, and give you a run for your money."

"No one gives me a run for my money," Jacob said.

Everyone laughed, and they all got to work, but late that afternoon, he sneaked out of the kitchen and headed to the conference level. There he found a long line of chef hopefuls in the hallway holding résumés in their fists, wearing eager expressions on their faces. He moved past them, ignoring the softly muttered grumblings when they thought he was cutting in line to get his shot at stardom.

Not a chance.

But as to why he was there, he couldn't have said. He honestly had no desire to be on a TV show, to be the "it" boy of the week, to have people watch his every move as if he were performing brain surgery.

He loved what he did too much to turn it into a spectacle. He loved all of it: the physical skills, the easy joy, the variety and the choices. It fed his heart and soul. And after too many years of being forced to prove himself, being evaluated at the blink of an eye, never knowing how long his job would remain his, he just couldn't imagine willingly putting himself there again, this time at the mercy of an intangible thing like ratings, or the invisible Powers-That-Be.

No, he was here merely to satisfy his curiosity and nothing else, and with that in mind, he walked to the double doors of their largest conference room.

Standing there was a man holding a radio and a clipboard.

Jacob recognized him as one of the two people who'd accompanied Em to dinner at Amuse Bouche two nights ago. "Eric," he said, remembering.

Eric looked up from the clipboard and raised a brow. "You want an audition?"

"No."

"So then why are you here?"

Hell if he knew. "Is Em inside?"

"Yep." But Eric stepped in front of him. "Sorry, man. Only people who are auditioning can get in there."

"I want to talk to Em."

"I don't think so."

"Why not?"

"Because whatever you've said or done to her already has left her feeling shaky. Now she's in there trying to save her career and I'm not going to have you screw with her head."

"You do realize she's the one who lied to me, right?"

"Not lied exactly," Eric corrected. "Just a slight omission is all."

Jacob raised a brow.

"Look, just leave her alone to do this, okay?"

"Are you her husband?" Jacob asked.

"What? No, of course not."

"Boyfriend?"

"No."

"Boss, then."

"No," Eric said, looking annoyed. "Not that it's any of your business."

"Then I'm going in."

"I already told you why you're not."

"Only if I was auditioning, right? Then you'd let me in."

Eric slapped the clipboard against his thigh as he

studied Jacob. "If you wanted to audition, none of this would have been necessary."

"I don't do performance cooking."

"Someone here in line today is going to be extremely thankful for that."

"I just want to talk to her."

Eric sighed. "You know what? Fine. Talk to her. But mess her up, and I'll mess you up."

They sized each other up for a moment, then Jacob sighed. "I'm not going to do anything to hurt her."

"Sure it's not too late for that?"

What the hell did that mean? Jacob had no idea, and with a muttered "thanks," he stepped inside the conference room. There was a long table set up, and behind it sat Em and a blonde, both watching the man standing in front of them.

The man was short, fat, bald and toting a whip. Instead of a white chef's hat and coat, he wore all black. "First, you must determine if the lettuce is dirty," he said in a deep, strict voice. He snapped the whip through the air for emphasis. "Is it dirty? Is the lettuce dirty? If so, naughty, naughty."

Jacob, who'd seen it all, just shook his head.

The blonde's mouth fell open.

Em looked equally flabbergasted.

"Are the tomatoes bad?" the auditioning chef asked sternly. "Are they very, very bad? If so, you slice them up real nice, or no food for you!" Another swoosh of the whip.

Em jerked to her feet. "Thank you," she said quickly. "That's enough."

The man pointed the whip at her. "You, quiet. I am not finished."

"Oh, yes, you are." Liza jumped up next to Em. "Get out."

The man "hmphed," then stormed past Jacob, his squat figure barely coming up to his shoulder.

The blonde reached for her drink. "Well, that was interesting."

"Yes," Em said, and looked at Jacob. Relief filled her gaze.

She thought he'd changed his mind, that he wanted to be her chef.

Jacob shook his head, and the disappointment in her eyes nearly killed him. It had been a hell of a long time since he'd disappointed someone he cared about.

It had been a long time since he'd cared like this at all.

Liza turned to see what had caught Em's eye, and put down her drink. "Tell me this is our lucky day," she said to Jacob.

Again he shook his head.

"You're killing me," Liza muttered. "*Next!*"

The doors opened. A woman entered, dressed in nothing but a string bikini. A string bikini with strings sorely tested by her considerable girth. Her large breasts were pushing precariously at their restraints, and the bottoms of the bathing suit were strained to the point of being frayed. She'd topped this off with pink polka-dot stilettos.

"My turn!" she cried, waving a carrot of all things. "I plan to be the Great Loss Chef! Together, me and America are going to lose twenty-five pounds!"

Jacob thought she could have tripled that and been closer to the right number.

She began gyrating, dancing to some music only she could hear, her body jiggling and shaking, and not in an attractive fashion.

"Uh, thank you," Em said. "But…"

The woman didn't stop. In fact, she kept dancing as she began to eat the carrot.

"That's all," Em called out politely.

"No, don't say stop," Bikini Woman pleaded. "I can do this! I'm your next amazing chef!"

"I'm sorry." Em shook her head. "I'm going to have to ask you to—"

"Not yet! I'm not finished—"

"Yes," Liza said firmly. "You are. *Next!*"

Bikini Chef threw her carrot to the floor. "This is nothing but a bunch of crap! I'm an excellent chef. You're all making a *big* mistake. You hear me? I was meant to be a star—my mother told me so!"

Em pressed her fingertips to her eyelids.

"Look," Em said firmly, dropping her hands. "You haven't shown me what I wanted to see, which was talent for cooking."

"That's because I can't cook," she cried.

"Then try one of the other reality shows," Em told her as patiently as she could.

Bikini Woman sighed, nodded and headed toward the

door. Once she was gone, Eric poked his head in. When Em shook her head to another contestant, he shut the door.

"It's going to be a hell of a long day," Liza said. She came around the table and eyed Jacob. "Unless you want to…"

Jacob shook his head.

Liza sighed. "Right." She glanced at Em, who hadn't taken her eyes off Jacob. "I'll give you two a minute. I'll just go get a coffee, maybe torture Eric with my beauty and wit."

"Liza—"

"Just kidding." She grinned. "Sort of. In any case, don't give me another thought."

When she'd left, Em said to Jacob, "Did you come for a good laugh?"

"I don't know, that S and M chef was…interesting."

She just shook her head. "God. I'm in big trouble."

"Maybe you should make a show of the auditions. A sort of preshow show. That'd be some good entertainment."

She laughed, only there wasn't much amusement in the sound, and he walked around the table to stand close to her. "You didn't really expect to find someone your first day."

She lifted her gaze to his and he saw the truth there. "You didn't expect to have to audition at all," he said.

She slowly shook her head.

"I'm sorry." He was shocked to find his apology genuine.

"I know." She smiled. "And it's okay. But if you're

not here because you've changed your mind, I need to get back to it." She gestured with her head toward the closed door, and the line of people waiting. "Just tell me there are no more whips or bikinis out there."

"No, but I did see a monkey."

She closed her eyes.

"And a set of triplets singing a cappella."

She opened her eyes again. "That's not funny."

"Not even a little bit?"

She tried to remain stern and unsmiling, but gave up. "A monkey? Ah, hell." She pinched the bridge of her nose. "Okay, yeah, maybe it is just a little bit funny. But it won't be next month, when I'm in the unemployment line."

Because he didn't want to picture that, he kept it light, leaning in to kiss her jaw. "I've got a plan to keep your mind off your troubles."

"I just bet." She eyed him warily but didn't pull away from his touch. "What is it?"

"Come out with me tonight after my shift."

"To…"

If he told her what he really wanted to do with her, to her, she'd probably pass out on the spot. "To see New York."

"I've seen the city."

"Come see it my way."

She was already shaking her head. "Ooooh, no. *Bad* idea."

"Actually, it's a great idea. It'll help you relax."

"Yeah? And how will being with you help me relax?"

He let out a slow grin, and she pointed at it, shaking her head. "Don't do that."

"Do what?"

"Turn on that charm. Because, damn it, I'd follow you anywhere when you smile at me like that, and that's bad. Very bad. I have a job to do, I have to—"

"You'd follow me anywhere?" he asked.

She looked at him for a long moment. "Let's just say, I have few survival skills when it comes to you."

He wasn't sure what to make of that, either, and suddenly he was uncomfortably warm. Was it hot in here? He took a step backward, toward the door, startled anew when she grabbed his hand, and at what he had in it.

Her note.

Unwrinkling it, she studied her own words. "I did promise to make it up to you," she said quietly, then lifted her face to his. "I guess I'll see you tonight."

Since he'd apparently lost his tongue, he couldn't come up with the words to tell her that she was right, this was a bad idea, that being with her wasn't good for his mental health.

Eric opened the door. "The natives are getting restless."

"Okay." Em smiled at Jacob. "See you later."

He looked into her beautiful face, with her thoughts chasing each other across her features. When he saw one particular thought—that she wanted him—he said softly, "Yeah, see you later."

HE WENT TO THE ONLY PLACE that ever made him feel better and completely at home.

His kitchen.

Pru was already there, brooding, too. After listening to her slam around in her wine cabinet for five tense, silent minutes, he sighed. "*What?*"

"You're not going to like it."

"Okay, then never mind."

She turned to him, her eyes wet, the emotion on her face stabbing directly into his heart. "I told Caya how I felt about her."

He backed up a step. "Okay."

"Yeah, that's what *she* said."

"What?"

Pru sighed. "She said okay. She said thank you. She said that it made her feel good. What she didn't say was 'I love you back, Pru.'"

"Why the hell would you tell her such a thing?"

"Because you told me to!"

"I told you to tell her you wanted her. I didn't say anything about love."

"But I do love her." Pru shut the cabinet hard enough that the bottles rattled, and crossed her arms, glaring at him as if this was all his fault.

"You scared her," he said.

"Take a peek into the dining room."

She tugged him to the kitchen door and cracked it open enough to reveal the front room. The waitstaff was out there having a meeting at one of the large dining tables. Caya was sitting on the lap of Michael, head-waiter. Her head was thrown back and she was laughing her cute ass off.

"Does that look scared to you?" Pru asked.

Uh, no, not exactly. He pulled Pru away from the door and looked into his usually calm friend's face. No calm there now. Just a panic he'd never seen before, and hurt. Damn it. Worse, looking at her expression, he saw something else. *Someone* else.

Em.

There had been pain in her eyes, too, and *he'd* put it there. "I tried to tell you this was a bad idea."

She let out a disbelieving sound. "That's it? That's all you've got? I told you so?"

"What else do you expect?" Honest to God, he didn't know. But he did know this: he had an ache in his chest that had better be heartburn and not emotion. What was wrong with everyone? Why couldn't it go back to the simplicity of before?

"Thanks, Chef," Pru said sarcastically. "Thanks ever so much."

"What do you want from me?" he asked helplessly.

"To make this better. Can you do that?"

If he couldn't help himself, how the hell did she think he could help her? "Pru…"

"Yeah, forget it." She sighed. "I'll be fine."

Jacob hoped so. And he hoped he'd be fine, too.

THE REST OF THE AUDITIONS were predictably horrible, but Eric promised Em they'd have a better selection tomorrow, and she chose to believe him rather than panic.

Tomorrow. Tomorrow her future would figure itself all out.

But first she had to get through tonight, and the evening with Jacob, without losing anything important.

Like her heart.

Nathan had called. Did she have him yet? She'd promised she was working on it and hung up.

Unable to find either Eric or Liza, she got ready alone, trying not to think too much.

Was she working on Jacob? No. She wouldn't do that. She couldn't. So what *was* it that she was doing?

She had no idea.

And what did one wear to go out on the town with Jacob Hill? She had no idea what to expect, much less how to prepare for it. Finally she settled for her favorite red cashmere hoodie, and a black skirt and boots. Comfort clothes that just happened to look decent enough for any adventure that came her way. Taking a peek in the mirror, she shrugged. Not bad, she supposed. *Hoped.*

He'd left her a message to meet him in the lobby at ten o'clock. She took the elevator, half expecting him to be on it already, where he'd start their evening off with a wild kiss.

But no Jacob.

Instead she rode the elevator with another couple who couldn't keep their eyes, mouths or hands off each other, leaving Em standing in the corner trying to pretend she couldn't see them, trying not to think about how she'd been kissed just like that woman was being kissed, trying not to remember what it had felt like to have Jacob's eyes, hands and mouth all over her.

She began to perspire.

God. The man could make her hot when he wasn't even anywhere near her. When the doors opened, she nearly ran off the elevator. Stepping into the lobby, her eyes locked on the life-size art deco painting of the threesome.

Perfect. Now even artwork was mocking her.

All around her, the place was hopping, people coming and going, some from Erotique, some from other areas of the hotel, others from the street.

Then she saw him standing in the center of the lobby, and everything else seemed to fade away. How cliché, how ridiculous, but the voices, the people, the sights and sounds, all of it vanished except for the sight of Jacob wearing all black, looking big, bad and extremely dangerous to her heart and soul.

And all she could think was…*God, I hope he kisses me again tonight. And touches me.*

And makes love to me.

The thought alone was enough to douse some of the excitement. No way. She was not going to sleep with him, not when she knew she was going to get on a plane in a matter of days and never see him again. She wasn't equipped for an affair.

Was she?

From across the lobby, through the people and the chatter of conversation and laughter, he smiled at her, one of his slow, heated smiles that rattled her knees and liquefied her bones.

Then he was walking toward her. With that long-legged stride and sense of purpose. Other women watched him, wanted him, and yet he didn't even look.

And despite what she'd told herself about her heart, it tipped on its side and began the fall.

"Hey," he said when he reached her side. He took her hand. "Ready?"

If he only knew just how ready she was, he'd go running into the night, putting as much distance between them as he possibly could. "Ready," she said, and put her hand in his. "Where are we going?"

"Anywhere. Everywhere."

He was true to his word. They walked through Soho, looking at art displayed on the street. Not pretty, neat museum art, but dark, deep stuff that she'd never experienced before, from artists who looked as if maybe they'd lived by train tracks their whole life, or out of cardboard boxes.

Jacob didn't say much, just waited for her reaction. She didn't know for certain but thought maybe this was his way of testing her—could she understand his world?

She studied the art, while Jacob studied her, appearing to be watching her for any signs of revulsion or discomfort, but she felt neither. In fact, with his big, tough body at her side, she'd never felt more comfortable, or safe.

And the art honestly captured her, entranced her. She told him so, and felt more than saw some invisible string of tension break free.

After that, he took her for a very late dinner at a tiny Thai place with only three tables, where no one spoke

English, where it was possible that everyone here had just gotten off a boat from Thailand. The place was clean but dark and furtive, as if the entire staff was ready to pick up and run at a moment's notice of the immigration authorities.

It was some of the best food she'd ever tasted.

It was Jacob, she knew, still trying to scare her off his world, which was so incredibly different from hers, but he didn't know that while she might look sweet and act sweet, even taste sweet, she could dig in her heels with the best of them. She didn't care that he'd had a vagabond, wanderlust life, and that hers had been relatively sheltered. She didn't expect anything more than what they could have in this moment right here, right now.

So the test continued.

They browsed through a magic shop for fun, then went through the back and ended up in a porn shop. Tasteful as the interior was, with lace and silk curtains dividing the DVDs from the whips and chains, Em still blinked in surprise. Dildos and vibrators and cock rings, oh my.

Jacob just watched her in that way he had of never hesitating, never fumbling, never looking flustered or confused.

God, to have half that confidence.

"Need anything?" he asked, deadpan.

"Um…" She eyed a row of anal plugs, each bigger than the last, and swallowed hard. "No, thanks."

"Sure?"

"Yes." She cleared her throat. "I'm good." She managed to look him in the eye. "You?"

For the first time all night, he tossed his head back and laughed, the sound real and rich and warming her belly.

And in that moment, she knew. Whether he liked it or not, whether he even knew it yet or not, she'd passed his test.

9

EM LOOKED AROUND HER at the porn shop. She was going to do it, she was going to buy something, just to see the look on Jacob's face when she did so with mature ease and without embarrassment.

Oh, he was standing there, so positive that he'd shocked her, so confident that she'd never have the guts to actually do it.

Ha! Watch her.

She stalked right up to the counter, telling herself she'd purchase the first thing she saw that she could name, heart racing at the selection of vibrators right in front of her. Gulping, she pointed to the one called The Rabbit—*the rabbit?!?*—and said, "That one."

Behind her, Jacob choked, but when she looked at him, he'd pulled himself together.

"Problem?" she asked loftily, taking out her credit card.

Jacob put his big, warm hand over hers and pulled out his wallet. "No way. This baby's on me." His eyes locked on Em's as he said to the woman behind the counter, "Add batteries."

Em was too mortified to argue with him, and the

next thing she knew, she was walking out of there with a brown bag heavy with The Rabbit, and a body zapping with sexual energy.

Unbelievable, but she was twenty-seven years old and had just bought her first vibrator.

"Don't worry, you'll like it."

"I wasn't worried."

His dimple flashed. "Were, too."

Damn it, did he have to read her mind, and then toss her own humiliating thoughts back at her?

He leaned in. "If you need any help with that thing, you just let me know."

Before she could formulate a response to this, he directed her into a bar.

A live band played with more decibels than talent, and the youthful, free-spirited crowd danced and laughed and talked over them. The servers wore jeans and suspenders—and no shirts. Including the women.

"Thought you could use a drink after that last adventure." Jacob gestured for the bartender, then looked at Em.

"A beer," she said, definitely needing it.

Jacob lifted up two fingers. When the drinks came, he looked at her over his bottle as he drank, his eyes filled with laughter and heat, God, so much heat.

She downed her beer. "I could probably use another."

"It's supposed to bring you pleasure," he said.

"The beer brought me plenty of pleasure."

"The vibrator."

"Oh."

"Gotta have trust, Em. There's easy pleasure there."

"Fine for a man to say. It's simple for you to—" She clamped her mouth shut. Had she just been about to say it, really? That it was easier for a man to masturbate?

Interested, he cocked his head. "What is it easier for men to do, Em?" His expression assured her she was still providing him with great entertainment. "Jerk off?" Leaning in so she could see nothing but that sinfully perfect face and yummy mouth, he whispered in an extremely naughty voice, "If you can't say it, how do you expect to be able to do it?"

"I can do it," she said, then wished she hadn't, because his grin widened.

"Sure?"

"*Yes.*"

"Because like I said, I could help—"

"I said I'd be fine! Now I need another beer. Please," she added in a more civil tone.

He tossed down the money to cover the beers they'd already consumed. "If it's serious drinking you're in the mood for, let's hit Patrick's."

She had no idea what exactly she was in the mood for, but it would be nice to assuage the odd ache deep inside her belly.

The one between her thighs was another story.

Patrick's was busy, too, with a very different crowd than the morning one. This crowd was tougher, younger, and looked far more apt to cause trouble. As they sipped their beers, Em noted that the trouble always seemed to be started by Maddie's two sons, who were bartending, when they weren't brawling.

After a lull in the noisy wildness, Jacob surprised Em by asking about the auditions.

"They went well," she said.

"Is that the line you gave your boss, or the truth?"

"The line I gave my boss." She sighed. "I'm hoping to get luckier tomorrow."

"And if you don't?"

"Maybe you'll change your mind."

"Em—"

"Just kidding." She shot him a half smile. "Sort of. Listen, what's so bad about being a TV chef anyway?"

"Other than the fact it's all a sham?"

"A sham?"

"Sure. The TV chef easily whips up some tasty-looking dish, impressing the viewers. He should, he's a trained pro. But you and I both know, due to time constraints and the boring factor, he'll skip all sorts of basic steps that the viewer has no idea how to perform, then tries it at home and experiences complete disaster trying to replicate it. I don't want to do that to people."

He'd really thought about this. "You wouldn't have to—"

"It's the advertising dollars that'll matter, or product placement, or something. Not the art of cooking."

She opened her mouth again, then slowly shut it in silent admission that it could be true.

"I'm just not interested," he said more gently. "At all. I've been there, done that, as far as cooking for performance, and I don't want to go back."

She nodded, remembering the juggling act he'd demonstrated. She knew how he'd grown up now and completely understood. And because she did, she would never want him to do this, either.

"So what are you going to do?"

She lifted her head with determination. "Hold auditions in Los Angeles. It'll give us more of a pool to choose from."

"Listen, I'm sor—"

Reaching out, she put a finger to his lips. "It's okay, I get it." And that was the thing, she really did. She knew Nathan wouldn't, but she did. "I'll make this work another way. I'm determined."

"You know," he said, watching her, "I believe you will."

"You do?"

"Oh, yeah." He stroked a finger over her jaw. "You've got something I recognize and know well."

Her breath caught at the touch. "What's that?"

"Determination. Passion. Hunger to succeed."

She understood him, and loved the feeling. But he understood her, too. Was there anything more sexy than that, a man who really knew her? She found herself fighting a broad, stupid smile. "You, Jacob Hill, are a very kind man."

He stared at her, then let loose with a laugh. "First you think I'm sweet, and now kind. Who are you looking at?"

"You."

"I'm not either of those things," he said with a slow shake of his head. "In fact, ask around." He shifted his weight on his bar stool, and suddenly his legs, long and hard were entangled, with hers.

Leaning in, he insinuated a muscled thigh between hers. His lips brushed against her ear as he spoke. "In fact, I'm probably the furthest thing from kind—or sweet—you'll ever meet."

His low, husky voice brought a set of shivers to her spine. But she couldn't think past the feel of his thigh between hers, or the hand he'd set against the bar at her back, ostensibly to hold his balance, but in reality trapping her within the confines of his body.

His gaze dropped to her mouth as he slowly pressed his thigh higher between hers. A rush of arousal surged through her. They were in public, anyone could see, and yet this excited her. She had no idea what that said about her, but she wanted more.

He moved again, just a slight shift that put him in direct contact with the V between her legs, shooting bolts of sexual yearning to every erogenous zone in her body. And apparently there were more than she'd known about.

No one around them paid any attention. And anyway, if anyone had happened to glance over, all they'd see was a couple who appeared to be in deep conversation, with his head bent attentively to hers, his arm at her back.

Then he rocked his knee again and she actually had to close her eyes, clutching the bar stool at either of her sides, seeking balance as everything within her clutched, as well. "I can't think when you do that," she whispered, and yet she didn't try to push his leg away.

"Do what?"

Her eyes flew open and she stared at him, prepared to tell him to stop teasing her, but he wasn't teasing at all. His eyes were dark, so very dark, and filled with honest curiosity.

He wanted to hear her say the words, that she couldn't think when he touched her, that she couldn't think with his thigh between hers, and that when he moved that thigh against her, she saw stars. Forget the vibrator, she wasn't going to need it.

"Em?"

Right. The words. Only she'd never been good at them. It was why she worked behind the camera and not in front of it, but she'd especially never been good with *sex* words. In the bedroom, on the rare occasion that she actually got there with a man, she was quiet, hoping he'd just guess what she wanted.

But suddenly she didn't want Jacob guessing. She didn't want to be coy. She wanted to be honest, and see where it got her. "I can't think when you touch me. When your leg is between mine, pressing against me."

Naturally he did it again, and her eyes drifted shut again. "Well, maybe I can think," she admitted softly. "But it's not the kind of thoughts made for mixed company."

"See, that's where you're wrong," he murmured in her ear. "Those thoughts spinning through your head *are* for mixed company. They're for me." He invaded her space a little more, making her suck in her breath because he felt so solid and smelled like heaven. "They're for you, too," he told her. "For what we do to each other."

She opened her eyes at that. "Which is what, exactly?"

"Make each other feel good."

Yes. Yes, she knew that, but she'd thought...for a minute she'd let herself think...hope... "Is there more than that?"

His gaze met hers. Again, openly honest. Brutally honest. "More than that isn't something I do."

"I know."

He looked at her for a long beat, then pulled back a little, and sipped at his beer, continuing to watch her thoughtfully. "How about you?"

"What?"

"You get involved with every guy you sleep with?"

"I'm afraid so, yes."

He nodded, and sipped some more, and by the way he'd backed off physically she got the message that he didn't intend to take it any further. Which in a strange way was a compliment.

He didn't want to hurt her.

But damn, she wished she'd let him take it a little further before they'd had that conversation, maybe even as far as his bed.

As if he could hear her thoughts, he smiled a little, and touched her hair, but he didn't try for more than that, and eventually they began the walk back to Hush. The streets were dark, quiet. There was no moon and a low fog lent an odd intimacy to the night around them.

The brown bag in her hands crinkled, reminding her of what she held.

And what she could do with it. "I can't believe I let you buy this for me."

The man beside her smiled but didn't speak. He never seemed to feel the need to fill an easy silence, and she'd gotten used to that. And nearly, but not quite, used to the way he touched her at every opportunity, a hand low on her spine as he guided her through a door, the way he bent close to her when he wanted to whisper something for her ears only, so that his jaw would brush hers and his lips graze the sensitive skin beneath her lobe.

"Tired?" he asked when they stood in Hush's lobby.

It was late, and given the stress of the few days she'd had here, she should have been past exhausted. But just peering into his dark, dark eyes banished any exhaustion. He was looking at her, his hands in his pockets, giving her an unusual amount of physical distance for a man who typically had no problem with body contact.

He was holding something back. Looking at him, she could see his shoulders tense with strain. His jaw was locked tight.

And that heat in his eyes was a carefully banked fire, and it nearly brought her to her knees.

He was holding back his desire for her.

Because of their conversation at Patrick's? If so, the man had been wrong about himself, he *was* sweet, and kind, so much so that she felt a lump catch in her throat.

He wasn't the type of man to let a woman close. He didn't want the burden or the responsibility of her feelings, much less his own. He'd learned young to count on no one but himself, and that wasn't a habit he would break lightly, if at all.

But she understood even more than that. This wasn't simply about her becoming attached to him.

But vice versa.

And he didn't like it. It scared him. That anything could scare this big, tough man was almost beyond comprehension.

But she'd scared him, and scared him deep. The tenderness that welled up nearly choked her.

"Why are you looking at me like that?" he asked, taking a step back, and she suspected, an even bigger mental one.

"Like what?" she asked softly.

His gaze searched hers. "Like maybe you're seeing me for the first time."

She was, and because of it, she smiled.

He did not. If anything, he looked more tense, and with his hands still in his pockets, the tendons and cords of muscle in his arms stood out in bold relief. The waistband on his pants gaped away from his flat, hard, tightened abs. She wanted to touch him there. Everywhere.

God, she wanted this man. She wanted to hold him, soften him, soothe him. She wanted to give him what he'd probably never let any woman give him: gentleness. Reaching up, she cupped his jaw.

He actually flinched. "What are you doing?"

"Touching you."

"Don't."

His voice sounded low, almost harsh, but she didn't take offense. Not when she'd just figured him out. "You touch me all the time," she told him. "Why can't I touch you?"

He didn't seem to have an answer for that.

So she smiled again and said, "Thank you for tonight, Jacob."

"I didn't do anything."

She lifted the brown bag. "You showed me a side of New York I might not have gotten to see."

His eyes darkened. The muscle in his jaw leaped. But he said nothing.

"I imagine it's still early for you," she said. "What are you going to do now?"

"I have to go up and look in on one of the suites. There's some VIP coming in tomorrow, and I'm cooking a private dinner for him and his fiancée. I want to check the kitchen."

"I heard the suites in this place are designer created and have to be seen to be believed."

He just looked at her.

She looked back, heart racing. What the hell was she doing? Baiting a tiger. Poking the bear.

"You want to come up to the suite with me," he stated rather than asked.

"Yes," she whispered quickly, before she changed her mind. She was insane, crazy—

"You know what toys the suites are equipped with?" he asked in a voice that left no doubt as to what category of "toys" he was referring to.

She'd read the brochures, and took a big gulp. "I think so."

"You think so." He shook his head and muttered something to himself that sounded like "Don't do it, Hill."

She just waited breathlessly.

He stared at her, the kind of deep, dark, edgy look that might have sent her running if it wasn't him. But she knew him now, and his bark was far worse than his bite.

At least she hoped so.

"There are video cameras and blank tapes," she said, "to be, um, used however the guest wants."

"They're not for filming the kids at the park."

"I know."

He stood toe to toe with her, not touching her in any way, but her body tingled nevertheless. "The camera is there to film the sex adventures the guests find here. Threesomes, hot tub adventures, S and M…"

She took another gulp. "I know. I want…I want to see."

"See? Or do?"

"I'm not sure yet."

He groaned at this, and turned in a slow, agitated circle, rubbing the day-old growth on his jaw.

The scratchy sound of it made her shiver. She wanted to feel it against her skin. "Show me," she whispered.

"I must be insane. *Insane*." He walked away a few feet, then stalked back, taking her hand. "Come on then."

He said this grimly, resignedly, and she wanted to tell him not to worry, it would be okay. But of course it wouldn't. Nothing would ever be okay again.

They took the elevator in silence, except for the brown bag in her hand, which crackled when she nervously tightened her grip.

Jacob's gaze met hers, and there was so much in it she swallowed hard. Before she could come up with something to say, he was leading her off the elevator and to the penthouse suites.

When he opened the door, she couldn't help but gasp. "Wow."

"Yeah." But he didn't seem to notice the surroundings as he nudged her inside enough to shut the door.

She gaped. She couldn't help it. The foyer was as large as her hotel room.

"It's called the Haiku Suite and was designed by Zang Toi. High-end Asian luxury."

There were floor-to-ceiling windows, and where there wasn't glass, the walls were upholstered in silk, the molding done in sycamore.

"The furniture is antique, the Oriental rugs hand-crafted." He shook his head. "It's amazing to me that someone would put such expensive stuff in a hotel, but people like to be pampered. Especially here."

She looked at the lovely antique furniture polished to a high shine and the low couches arranged in a way that encouraged socializing. "There's still something different…"

He turned and looked at her. "Do you mean because it's meant for sex?"

"Um…" She bit her lower lip and clutched her brown bag. "Well, yes."

"You don't know the half of it." He pointed to an enclosed bookcase. "There's the video selection. Let me be specific. We're talking erotica. The best out there. Specifically designed for each guest." He pulled open the doors and revealed a stack of DVDs all geared toward spanking. "This particular guest's favorite fantasy."

She swallowed hard. "Um, how does Hush know what they'll want?"

"Questionnaires."

"The questions must be interesting."

"You know it." He pulled out a DVD. The cover showed a woman over a man's knee, her skirt pushed high on her waist, her panties to her knees, her bottom extremely red.

She struggled not to react but she felt her eyes widen.

"What do you think?" Jacob asked her, sounding darkly amused.

She looked at the man's big hand, raised above the woman's bottom. "Um…"

"Let me guess. Not your cup of tea?"

"Not quite," she managed.

With a rough laugh, he put the DVD back and took her into the bedroom, opening the closet there.

This time her mouth just fell open.

"A selection of costumes," he said, holding up a leather bustier, complete with whip. "This one is for a dominatrix fantasy." He arched a brow at her choked laugh. "No?"

"No," she said, shaking her head.

He pulled out another hanger. "How about a French maid?"

"Uh…no. Thank you."

Shrugging, he put that one back and opened the

chest at the foot of the luxurious bed. Inside was a selection of...oh, my.

More toys, some of which she couldn't even identify.
"Quite the education," she managed, leaning over him,
touching a set of what she assumed were hand and ankle
cuffs, in braided leather, lined with fur. She caught his
eyes and nearly stopped breathing.

He was watching her finger the handcuffs, his eyes
so dark she couldn't differentiate the iris from the
pupil. "Well?"

"I've never...um."

He lifted a brow.

"I've never been bound before," she whispered.

"A fantasy?" he asked, his voice a mere whisper of
a breath.

She touched a set of silk scarves, a leather harness,
a riding crop, and shivered. "I didn't think so..." But
now she could see herself bound in the cuffs, the scarf
over her eyes, her body stretched to its limit on the
bed as he leaned over her, taking her to helplessly
aroused heights....

"Jesus, Em." Backing away from the closet, he
shoved his fingers through his short, short hair, heat
and sexual frustration coming off him in waves. "I'm
just a man here."

Yeah. She was counting on that.

He turned toward the bathroom, which was bigger
than her condo at home. An open sitting area sported a
set of cushy, leather massage tables side by side.

"Wow," she murmured.

"You've said that."

She looked at him. He had carefully kept his distance, which in itself was extremely telling. Setting her brown bag down on the flawless polished granite counter, she nodded to the massage tables. "For couples?"

"You can get a masseuse in here, or just do each other. Everything needed is in the cabinets at the side of the tables."

She opened one and saw oils, lotions, candles… "I used to do manicures," she said. "I gave the best hand massages in Hollywood."

A dimple flashed. "I'm not going to touch that one."

She just gave him a long look.

"And here I thought you were just a producer."

"Now." And hopefully also next month. "But when I was in college, I worked wherever the money was. People gave great tips for my hand massages." She patted a lounge chair. "I could show you."

He stayed across the room, his hands in his pockets. "I don't think so."

And the hunter became the huntee. This was too good to pass up. "Chicken?"

His eyes reflected how he felt about being called a chicken, and she nearly backed off. And she would have backed off if she hadn't seen other things there as well, like—it couldn't really be—uncertainty?

And want. There was no mistaking that one.

Good Lord, it was the sheer magnitude of that want that had her trying again to reach him. "Sit," she said again. "Try it." *Try me.*

He hesitated for one beat, then strode over to her and did as she'd asked, sitting on one of the massage tables. "Turnaround is fair play," he said so silkily she got goose bumps.

"You mean you want to massage my hands, too?" she asked.

"Not your hands, no."

Oh, boy. She took his wrists and turned them. Ran her thumbs over the work-roughened skin and calluses of his palms. "You haven't been moisturizing."

"No," he agreed, his gaze still locked on her face.

"Your hands are your treasure, Jacob."

"Actually, I think of my treasure as another body part entirely." Another flash of that dimple. "Want to moisturize and massage that part?"

10

To: Chef
From: Deidre
Hey, I'm at Exhibit A having way too much fun.
Nothing you're doing can possibly compare, so
get your gorgeous ass down here and join me.

EM SWALLOWED HARD and looked into Jacob's challenging eyes. "Let's start with your hands," she managed.

She had the pleasure of seeing those eyes glaze over, of watching *him* swallow hard, of rendering *him* speechless for a change.

About time.

The sheer womanly power of it made her want to toss her head back and laugh. Or rip off all her clothes and offer herself to him.

She did none of those things, just smiled in what she hoped was a daringly sexual way, and reached for a bottle of oil from the cabinet. She poured a little on her palm, its mixed scent sweetening the air. Then she reached for his hands and began to rub them.

At first, he remained silent, though she could feel him

looking at her. She dug in, taking her time, hitting every muscle, every tendon, working each finger, his palm, his thumb. "Good?" she finally murmured, lifting her head.

His eyes were dark, his face taut as he gestured with his chin. She followed his gaze down.

He was unmistakably hard, the proof of it pressing against the buttons of his black Levi's.

Yep. It was good.

"My turn," he said thickly when she was done.

Oh, boy. He rose from the table and eyed her in a way that had her backing up. "You know what? That's okay," she decided. "My hands are good. I don't work them nearly as hard as you work yours—"

"Get on the table, Em."

"Well, I—"

"Chicken?"

She looked into his daring eyes, reminding herself she'd wanted this. She'd egged him on, played the game, and now she was going to follow through. "Okay, fine." She sat primly, legs swinging off the sides, hands in her lap. "I'll have you know, massaging hands takes quite the technique, not everyone can—"

"I'm not going to massage your hands. Lie down."

"Um—"

He clucked like a chicken, and she had to laugh. "Fine." She wasn't afraid of him.

Or not much, anyway.

Swallowing again, she contemplated the situation and tried to decide whether to lie facedown or faceup, because if she went facedown she couldn't see what he was up to, but if she went faceup then that left him with some fairly obtrusive areas to touch....

"You're thinking too much again," he said, sounding amused. At her expense.

"Yeah." Was that her voice, all breathless and wispy? Good Lord. She shut her mouth and lay down. Facedown. Then she scrunched her eyes shut and pretended she was Alice, going down the rabbit hole.

"I'm not sure what you think I'm going to do to you." He still sounded quite amused as she felt him slip off first one of her shoes and then the other. "But if you want to be nervous, go ahead and be nervous." His hands slid beneath her long skirt to her calves, massaging lightly over her tights. "I'll promise you this, though."

My God, his hands were heaven, she thought dazedly as he dug into her calf muscles with a gentle firmness.

Leaning over her, he spoke into her ear in that voice that could bring her to climax all by itself. "You're going to like it. You're going to like it so much you'll be begging me for more."

Even if that were true, she'd never admit it. "I never beg."

He only slid his hands farther, past the backs of her knees.

"Uh—"

"Shh." Still higher his hands went, until his fingers hooked the elastic edging of her tights and tugged.

"Jacob—"

"I want to touch bare skin." After stripping the tights down her legs, he dropped them to the floor. She watched them hit and told herself he'd seen her far barer than this. Just as she also told herself he was going to take liberties that she wasn't altogether sure of, liberties that would put her far past her comfort level.

But everything about this man took her past her comfort level and she couldn't seem to get enough.

"Relax," he said, reaching for the oil.

Right. She'd just relax.

BOTTOM LINE FOR JACOB, he was fascinated by Em and her layers: the way she loved her friends, the way she'd responded with empathy to the story of his childhood, the way she'd laughed when he'd gotten silly and showed off his juggling skills.

Everything about her drew him, and that was quite possibly the most unsettling thing he'd ever felt, because it left him wanting more, more of her, more of this.

More of them.

Just the thought made him wish he had a drink, a hefty one, when he no longer drank the hefty stuff. What the hell had happened to a woman being just like a recipe, something to try and then move on to the next?

Nothing, he assured himself. He was just playing here, and so was she. To make sure of it, he poured the scented oil in his hands, slicked them up and touched her, because touching her made him forget everything else.

He started with her feet, pressing into the arches, rubbing all of the tension out, working his way over her ankles to her calves, which were smooth and creamy. This California girl didn't tan. She had her legs pressed tightly together, her muscles working overtime to keep them so. For whatever reason, that made him smile as he slowly worked his way past her knees, beneath her skirt to the backs of her thighs.

He wasn't kidding before. He knew exactly how good he was with his hands, and before much longer, he expected her to cave, and he expected her to beg.

Her soft, helpless moan swiped the smile right off his face, jerking him out of his smug complacency. She was right on schedule and yet he hadn't expected the sound to reach him.

Nor had he expected that having his hands beneath her skirt, out of view and yet on her bare skin, would seem like the most erotic thing he'd ever seen.

Her muscles were knotted and he worked them, dragging yet another moan from her. Utterly arousing.

"Shh," he said, not ready to give in to it, in to her.

But as he pressed the knotted muscles high on her thighs, she squirmed and then shifted slightly, her legs no longer pressed so tightly together, allowing him better access.

He took the opportunity, skimming his fingers higher, then higher again so that they just touched the elastic edging of her panties.

Silk.

Aw, man, they were silk and flimsy. One little tug and he'd rip them free. Because he couldn't actually see them, he wondered what color they were. Black? Red?

She lay on the table utterly motionless, holding her breath, he guessed, and slowly—so slowly he had to grit his teeth—he traced the edging of the panties to the string over either hip.

String bikini. His favorite.

"What color?"

"Wh-what?"

He almost didn't recognize his own hoarse voice. "What color are they?"

She remained still for a beat, then let out a breathless laugh that shook her shoulders. "I can't remember."

He ran his finger over the very tops of them now, drawing a line low on her spine.

Her breath caught. "They might be peach."

Now it was his turn to hold his breath.

"Or black." She said this in a whisper.

His body tightened. His fingers wrapped around the material of her skirt and slowly pushed it up, past her knees, revealing a gorgeous set of legs he wanted wrapped around him. Her thighs were every bit as taut and creamy smooth as he remembered from the spa, and his mouth went dry.

Then he pushed the skirt up even farther, to her waist now, and exposed her ass, covered in a silky pair of barely there bikini panties.

Black.

His heart was drumming in his ears, all the blood in his head draining south. Reaching out, he traced his finger over her hip, then curled his finger around the string.

She squirmed again.

One yank, he thought, just one yank… His knees actually wobbled.

"It's…warm in here," she murmured very softly, making him realize he'd been staring down at her like a sixteen-year-old virgin with his first glimpse beneath his girlfriend's dress.

Hell, he felt like a damn virgin, a clumsy one. "You're wearing a sweater."

"I could take it off…"

Great idea. Reaching up, he pulled the sweater over her head.

Beneath, she wore a pale pink camisole, spaghetti straps, one of which had slipped off her shoulder. He nudged the other one, helping it to the same position, absorbing her caught breath, getting a surge of possessive desire at the sight of her flat on her belly, gripping the sides of the table, her shirt shoved high, straps off her shoulders, face turned away.

God. He had to stand there and purposely drag air into his lungs. Massage. He was here to give her a massage, and drive her as crazy as she drove him.

And to make her beg. Let's not forget that. Teeth clenched, he poured more oil into his hands, and with her skirt still bunched at her waist, worked on her bared shoulders, dragging more soft moans from her. "How are you doing?" he murmured, moving inward, to the back of her neck.

"Mmm," was her only answer, so he took his hands down her shoulder blades, and when the top of the camisole got in his way, he merely tugged it down to her waist.

On her belly, gripping the edges of the table for all she was worth, she gasped.

He smiled grimly and went back to work.

After a stiff moment, she let out a breath and relaxed into his touch, and when he'd removed every bit of tenseness from as much of her back as he could reach, he leaned in, kissed her jaw, and said, "Turn over."

Her eyes flew open. "Um—"

"Unless, of course, you're afraid I'll actually do it."

"Do what?"

"Make you beg."

She squeezed her eyes shut again for a beat.

This was it, he thought with mixed feelings of relief and regret. He'd pushed her past her boundaries. She was going to tell him to take a flying leap. She was going to run back to her room, then back to Los Angeles, certain she'd met the worst of the worst.

And then she did the unthinkable.

She turned over.

She bared her body, and given the way her eyes held his, open and vulnerable, she bared her heart and soul, as well.

Shit, he thought, feeling something deep inside him give. Crack. Break.

Desperately afraid it was his heart, he shoved it out of his thoughts by letting his gaze gobble her up. And there was a hell of a lot to gobble; the woman was a walking wet dream. Her bare breasts were perfect handfuls. No, make that perfect mouthfuls, with their soft curves and rosy nipples, hardening for him into two tight buds that made his jaw ache because he was holding it so tight.

Her ribs rose and fell quickly with her accelerated breathing, and though her camisole and skirt blocked a strip of her belly, he could see enough to know that it was softly rounded and pale and so smooth he wanted to rub his jaw right there.

Just below her bunched-up skirt were those heart-stopping panties. Black. Silky. And riding high enough to fully outline her.

His little L.A. producer was waxed or shaved or whatever mysteries it was that a woman did there. Her long, long shapely legs beckoned, and he ran a hand up one, feeling her tremble. "Cold now?"

Eyes never leaving his, she shook her head.

Holding her gaze, he added his other hand, dancing his fingers up both her thighs, past her panties, skirt and camisole, settling his palms on her ribs.

Again her breath caught, an audible sound in the room.

He stroked over her flawless skin, the very tips of his fingers just barely brushing the undersides of her breasts.

Her nipples tightened even more.

She licked her lips, swallowed hard, but kept looking at him, even when he shifted his hands, gliding them up to cup her beautiful breasts in his palms.

"Oh," she breathed, startled.

His thumb brushed her distended nipples, then he bent his head to take one into his mouth.

Arching her back, she gripped the sides of the table and let out a soft, erotic hum.

And he was a goner. Lifting his head, he looked down at her, then put his mouth to her jaw, her ear, inhaling her, the scent of her shampoo, her skin. Had he really believed he could just tease her, tease himself, and then walk away without sinking into her body? "Em…"

Her eyes fluttered open, filled with heat and need and something that nearly brought him to his knees.

Affection. Her eyes were swimming with it.

So he closed his and concentrated on the intoxicating scent of her, the feel of her glorious body. "We're going to do this."

"Yes," she shocked him by saying, reaching up, fisting her hand in his shirt, holding him over her, leaving him no choice but to look deep into her eyes. "Now. Please, now."

As if he could possibly resist. Bending, he kissed the heavy underside of her breast, licked his way to her nipple, and sucked it into his mouth.

Crying out, she arched up again, reaching for him, her warm hand running up his torso and then down again, her fingers tracing the ridges of his ab muscles.

With her breast in his mouth, her nipple pebbling against his tongue, and her hand warm and soft beneath his shirt now, he couldn't have walked away to save his life. She murmured his name on a sigh as her hand stroked over his bare belly now, then lower, toying with the waistband of his jeans.

It was both heaven and hell. Heaven because touching her like this, looking at her, felt so good. Too good. Hell because he already knew one time with her would never be enough.

Knowing it, pushing it out of his mind, he slid his hand down the length of her arm, twining his fingers with hers, lifting her hand over her head so she couldn't keep touching him, because if she did, this was going to be over before it started. Apparently with her, he couldn't control himself. So he took her other hand, pulling it out from beneath his shirt, bringing it up, as well, squeezing lightly.

Her response was a rocking of her hips, a soft wordless plea, which he answered with a kiss. Leaning over her, he opened his mouth on hers and claimed her as his.

Hot, wet, deep, the kiss said it all, sending waves of need and desire to pool behind the buttons on his Levi's.

"Jacob," she whispered into his mouth, her breath sweet and hot, the little catches in her throat the sexiest thing he'd ever heard, making him forget the suite, his job, her job, the reason they'd even met, making him forget everything but how soft and giving her mouth was, her tongue just a little shy until he coaxed her with his. It was a kiss that left him wanting a hell of a lot more than what he could get in this position.

He broke contact, his body hardening even further at her low, mewling protest. Moving around from the side of the massage table to the foot, he put a hand on each of her hips and tugged, bringing her up flush against him, her legs sprawled, her black silk-covered crotch snug to his denim-covered one.

Blinking up at him, she smiled, and if his heart hadn't clutched hard before, it did now. She sat up and reached for his shirt, pulling it over his head, tugging him forward to catch his mouth with hers while her fingers danced over his flesh, making his muscles jerk and bunch with each stroke over his chest, over his stomach, then lower.

Again she toyed with his waistband, and this time didn't stop there, but pulled hard until the first button popped open. And then the next.

His body surged; his toes curled. He was going to lose it before they'd even started, something that had never happened, even when he'd been young and extremely stupid. He was quickly spiraling out of control here, wanting nothing more than to sink hard and fast into her body, forget finesse.

Again he bent over her, pressing her back to the table, stroking his hands up the undersides of her arms, bringing them back over her head, leaning down to kiss her long and hard, until he felt her writhing against him, until she was panting with the need for more, until she was lost in the passion. There. He had her now. He trailed hot, wet, open-mouthed kisses down her torso, flicking his tongue over one nipple, then the other, swirling past her belly button, past the bunched-up clothes in his way.

Standing between her legs as he was, she couldn't close them, but given how she wrapped them around his hips, she didn't seem to want to. He curled his fingers into the elastic strip of her bikini panties and tugged.

They ripped free.

At the sound of the silk giving way, she blinked up at him, and he thought, *Now I've finally pushed her too far and she'll shove me away.* He was even braced for it, the apology ready on his tongue.

Instead she arched up again, her bare flesh against his denim, and whispered, "Oh, please."

He looked down to where her legs were opened, wrapped around his hips.

She was wet, and at the sight he groaned, slipping a finger into her.

Her breath came in short, desperate pants that went into overdrive when he added a second finger, slicking his thumb over ground zero.

"Jacob." She sounded panicked, her hips oscillating. "Please…"

"Come," he murmured, watching his fingers sink in and out of her creamy heat. "I want you to."

She brought her hands down and gripped his, holding his thumb to the right spot, and as she cried out and began to shudder, he bent over her and drew a nipple into his mouth.

It seemed to draw out her climax, or restart it. Watching her, listening to her, feeling her, made him crazy for her. While she was still lost in the throes, he shoved his jeans to his thighs and grabbed a condom from the still-opened drawer.

She opened her eyes and wrapped her fingers around the biggest, hardest erection he'd ever had, leaving him to stifle his groan as he helplessly pushed into her hand. She squeezed, and stroked him, and somewhere in the back of his mind he recognized that she was wrestling his control from him again, and that he was powerless to stop her this time. Everything she was doing, every touch, every sound she made, every look she gave him, drove him closer and closer, until he was standing on the edge.

She leaned in and kissed his pec, stroking him, and again his hips rocked to meet her, a base reaction he could no more have stopped than his next breath. Too good, this felt too good, and he was too far gone to be teased. He wanted to be inside her when he came. "Em."

Her busy fingers were exploring him, and there was a sexy little catch in her throat as she touched his body, as she looked up at him with everything she felt in her eyes. "Hurry, hurry, hurry," she said. "Oh, please, hurry."

It was all far too much for his poor, aching body. Unbelievable as it seemed, she was going to take him right over the edge with nothing more than her touch. *"Wait."* He heard the shocking desperation in his own voice. Later he could kick himself for letting it get so out of hand.

For now he tore open the condom packet and did his best to get it on.

Her fingers covered his. "You're shaking," she murmured.

Yeah. Shaking. *Shaken.* To the bone.

Pulling his head down, she smiled into his eyes, tugged a little harder and kissed his tense jaw. He figured if he got any more tense his teeth would shatter.

Then she kissed her way to his ear. "I love your body," she whispered, and gave a damp lick to his lobe, along his throat.

He groaned. She was going to devour him. Kill him. *"Em."*

"I know," she murmured softly, soothingly, cupping his face, touching her forehead to his.

Christ. Tenderness. He didn't want tenderness. It brought a shocking lump to his throat, and made his eyes burn. Unable to handle either, he pushed her back to the table. Grabbed her hips. Gave a hard yank so that her wet heat slid over him, making his vision double and his knees wobble again. "Hold on," he grated out. "God-damn it, hold on to me."

But she already was, and as he thrust hard into her body, she cried out, a sound of pleasure, of surprise, of need, her groan mingling with his.

"Kiss me," she whispered, and he did, leaning over her, thrusting inside her again as his mouth touched hers.

Her body tensed. "Jacob…"

"Again," he demanded. "Come again," he growled, holding on to her as she did just that, his name a sigh on her lips.

He was lost then. Lost in her body, in the feel of her, lost in her eyes.

Even as he was found.

11

MUCH LATER, JACOB WALKED Em to her hotel room. She didn't know what she expected but it wasn't for him to follow her inside.

The light on her phone was blinking, so she picked it up to retrieve her messages, feeling a little self-conscious and a lot aware of the big, bad, silent man behind her, watching her every move.

What they'd just shared had been so intense, she didn't know how to react. Just remembering how she'd cried and panted, and damn it, *begged*, had the heat rushing to her face. Plus she was fairly certain she'd embedded her fingernails in his most excellent posterior, which meant that he had ten indentations in there.

Did he even know? If he didn't, surely he realized she'd bitten him on the shoulder in those last few seconds, when she'd practically burst out of her own skin. She'd left teeth prints; she'd seen it herself when he'd put his shirt back on.

God. She'd turned into a wild animal.

She had no idea how she was going to look him in the eyes ever again. *You won't have to tomorrow, when you leave.* Her heart clenched at that but she ruth-lessly shoved the thought aside as she accessed her messages. She had two, the first from a desperate-sounding Eric.

"Your assistant has lost her mind," he hissed. "She's pounding on my room door, wanting in. Do you hear her?"

Indeed Em could hear some sort of knocking.

"I can see her through the peephole," Eric said des-perately. "And good Christ, you should see what she's wearing. Nearly nothing, if you're wondering!" His voice cracked. "I know I promised you I'd resist her but that was when she was drunk. She's not drunk now, and I don't think I'm going to stay strong, Em. Either call me and remind me why I'm not having sex with her, or don't be upset at the consequences."

Click.

Em stared at the phone and made a sound of worry. She'd wanted them to get back together, but only if they were both ready. The past few days had told her Liza wasn't, and might never be. The fool.

"What's wrong?" Jacob asked.

"Nothing." Except her best friend was going to gobble up her other best friend, and then spit him out like yesterday's trash. It was Liza's MO: love them and leave them before they did the same to her.

Until Eric, no one had ever gotten hurt.

But now Liza had the poor man ensnared for the second time. Eric had a heart of gold behind all that sar-castic wit, and Em was worried.

The next message was Liza herself. "Don't bother

coming down here and saving him," she said. "I've got him right where I want him, and let me just say all these toys in the closets here at Hush are coming in handy."

Em listened to this and felt the impending train wreck.

"I've found some silk scarves in the armoire here, and I don't think they're meant to wear for a walk in the park. I've got him tied to the bed. He's a willing captive, though, so don't worry. I'm going to take good care of him."

Click.

Em hung up the phone and told herself they were both grown-ups. They could handle the consequences…

"Em?"

She turned to Jacob, and while she didn't quite manage to look him in the eyes, she settled her gaze on his chest. "Liza has Eric tied up in his room. Literally."

His eyes heated.

In response, something happened deep in her belly. To cover the confusing reaction, she laughed a little nervously. "What is it about this place? It brings out the animal in people."

"Is that what you think happened upstairs?" His voice was as intoxicating as whiskey. "The ambience got to us?"

"I'm not sure," she admitted.

He came toward her, tossing her brown bag onto the table—she'd nearly forgotten her purchase!—and put his hands on his hips as he looked at her and said, "Again."

"Wh-what?"

"Again," he said, and made her nipples hard and her panties wet.

Yes. Oh, yes, she wanted him again.

And again.

But he was talking about right here, right now. She also wanted him tomorrow. And the next day. And, she was beginning to realize, the tomorrows after that.

But what did he want? Certainly not that kind of tie, and knowing it should have given her pause, should have stopped her.

It didn't.

Her heart nearly burst as she tossed her room key aside and flung herself at him, sighing with pleasure when he caught her up in his arms. She could feel the barely restrained need in him, and thought maybe, just maybe, he wanted more, too.

It was enough for her.

"Let me," he said, dodging her fingers when she reached to get his shirt off. Instead he kissed her until she was dying for more, holding her hands behind her back while he decimated her with his mouth, his hands, his body.

"Let me," he whispered again, when finally, finally, he stripped her down to her skin. This time, he murmured with pleasure over every inch he uncovered, taking the time to touch her, to taste her.

And then he just took her, which he did in the hot tub.

"Again," he repeated later when he took her on the counter.

Then the rug on the floor.

And then even later, on the chair by the window overlooking the bright lights of the city that never sleeps.

They finally fell onto the bed somewhere around three, where Jacob pulled her against his warm, hard body and fell instantly asleep.

She stared into his face, relaxed as he slept, and felt her heart click into place. She could love this man. She could love him forever, if he'd let her.

But she already knew he wouldn't. He might think he'd kept the reins tight on his emotions tonight, hiding from her how he was starting to feel, hiding his fear of letting go, of giving her control and losing his, but he hadn't really kept a thing from her.

A surge of emotion for him welled up and filled her heart and her eyes. Leaning in, she put her lips softly to his. "'Night," she whispered.

He hummed in pleasure and tightened his grip on her without waking all the way. With a dreamy sigh, she snuggled in and let sleep claim her, too.

AN ALARM WENT OFF and Jacob jerked awake. He was in a bed, a strange bed, with a delicious, warm, naked female body plastered to his side.

Not just any bed, and not just any woman.

Hush.

Em.

He had a handful of breast with a nipple pebbling in his palm, his other hand cupping a warm buttock. *Nice.* Rumbling approval deep in his throat, he rolled her to her back, settling his weight on her, thrusting a thigh high between hers to spread her for his pleasure.

"The alarm," she gasped.

Reaching out, he knocked the clock to the floor and it went mercifully silent.

"Auditions," she mumbled, eyes still closed. "I have to— *Ohmigod.*"

Having sucked a nipple into his mouth, he teased the tip with his tongue, smiling at her moan, at the way she clutched at him with her hands, her legs.

"Jacob—"

Lightly he bit down on her nipple, then flicked it with his tongue.

Her fingers dug into the muscles of his shoulder, her body arching up into him.

Oh, yeah. Good. His slid his hand down her side, spreading his fingers wide to touch all that he could, her ribs, her belly, her hip. "Wait," she gasped.

He palmed her sweet ass, then dipped his fingers in— "*Jacob.*"

For the first time he heard the tone in her voice. The reluctant tone. The tone he'd used often enough the morning after when he'd had enough of a woman and needed out.

That was when he woke all the way up and smelled the news.

She was done with *him.*

She was done with him before he'd been done with her. That had never happened, not once, and a feather could have knocked him over he was so shocked.

"Right." Without looking into her eyes, he rolled off her and off the bed all in one move. Reached for his jeans.

"Jacob."

Where the hell were his shoes?

"Jacob."

"Don't get up," he said, shoving his legs into his jeans and grabbing his shirt. "I know my way out."

Did he ever. He always knew his way out, and was pissed he'd stayed.

Sex with a woman, he could do that. He knew how to do it, extremely well.

Sleeping with one, not so much. In fact, he rarely did it at all, and never on a woman's turf.

Seems he'd broken all his own rules last night.

That's what he got for thinking with the wrong head.

The paper bag on the dresser mocked him. It was open, the packaging of the vibrator strewn over the glossy wood.

They'd put that thing to some fun, sexy, outrageous use, and if his heart hadn't been pounding heavily, uncomfortably, the memories of what they'd done would have made him smile.

As it was, they made him hard.

Because after her initial shyness, Em had gotten into it. Very into it. The batteries were close to dead.

Damn, he was thinking again.

He made it to the door before he felt her hand on his arm, trying to tug him around. He stared at his own hand on the handle. "Don't, Em."

"Look at me," she said softly, her hand rising to glide over his back. He felt his muscles quiver at the touch.

"Please?" she whispered.

Gritting his teeth, he turned only his head and met her eyes. They were deep and full not of discomfort or irritation at him still being here but hope and joy and, damn, that knee-knocking affection again.

She hadn't run off like a scared little bunny at the depths of his passion. Hadn't run from anything he'd shown her, as he'd assumed—and half hoped—she would. He didn't understand what drew him to her, why he suddenly wanted to toss her back into that bed and follow her down, why he wanted to keep her.

Keep her.

He couldn't keep her. Even thinking it was the stupidest thought he'd ever had. He'd never managed to keep anything in his life, not a place, not a thing, and sure as hell not a person.

"Last night," Em said, searching his gaze for something, God knew what. "It was…different."

He let out a harsh laugh. "Yeah. I'm guessing not a lot of guys would take you to a porn shop."

"That wasn't all that was different."

"You probably don't do a lot of barhopping, either. At least the kind of bar I took you to."

"I didn't mean different bad." She looked at him as if she could see right through him, damn it, into the very black depths of his soul. "I meant different…scary."

Scary? He'd scared her? Christ. "Em…" He squeezed his eyes closed tight. "I didn't mean to… I wouldn't—"

"No." She turned him to face her, both hands on his arms. "No." She smiled. "Scary good. I'm trying to tell you that I had the most amazing time, and yes it was different, and yes it scared me because it was different. Different as in more meaningful. What we shared last night when we made love—"

"Wait." He shook his head. God, he couldn't let her finish. "I think you should stop right there. Before you say something you're going to regret in the name of lust."

"It wasn't just lust."

"Yes," he said. "It was. It was just a normal night of lust."

"Oh." She blinked once, the hurt in those depths unmistakable. "I see."

Hell. He should have left last night. He was a complete idiot. "I don't want to hurt you—"

"No. No, it's okay. I understand. It was a casual thing."

"That's right. Just a normal night out—"

"I get it." She nodded. She took her hands from his arms. Backed up a step. Even curved her mouth into a smile.

Though it didn't come close to reaching her eyes.

"Don't worry," she said, trying to soothe him, which made him feel even more like slime. "I'm fine."

From somewhere behind them her cell phone rang and she jerked as if she'd been shot. "Excuse me, I've got to get that—"

"Yeah. Uh…good luck with your auditions." At his own lame words, he winced. *Good luck?* Could he be a bigger ass? "Em—"

But she'd already turned away.

Just as he'd wanted.

EM PICKED UP her ringing cell phone. When she heard her hotel room door close behind Jacob, she closed her eyes. He was gone…

Just a normal night out.

She was such a fool, such a damn fool, she thought angrily as she flipped open her phone. "Hello?"

"Em."

"Eric." She let out a breath and concentrated on the here and now. "I take it you're not still…tied up."

"Uh, no." He lowered his voice. "Look, it was great. But…"

"But what?"

"Afterward…" He sighed. "She cried, Em. It broke my heart."

"Why are you whispering?"

"Because she's asleep right next to me. Why did she cry?"

Em sank to the bed. "Did you ask her?"

"She denied doing it, but I saw the tears."

"What happened after that?"

"We, uh, did it again. It was…well, words fail," he said in an awed voice. "Not the sex, the connection, you know?"

Yeah. She knew.

"I fell in love with her all over again."

Em let out a long breath. She was falling, too.

"God," Eric whispered. "I think she's just screwing with my head. What do I do?"

She laughed a little harshly. "Eric, what in our history

together makes you think that I have any clue when it comes to love?"

"Because your heart's always in the right place. You're all about heart and soul, Em, making memories, shit like that."

"Yeah, well, I'm really a pretty big screwup in that area. Right now all that matters is that we're going to be unemployed and eating canned soup for the rest of our lives if I don't get downstairs and get going on the auditions—"

"She cried, Em."

Em rubbed her aching temples. Other things ached, too. Between her thighs.

But the biggest ache of all came from her heart, which she reached up and rubbed now, though it didn't help. "If I had to guess, she cried because she loves you, too."

Utter silence greeted this.

"Eric? You there?"

"She told me she doesn't."

"Even you are not that clueless as to believe her."

"Look, I'm just a guy," he pleaded. "We were *born* clueless."

"Okay, listen, I haven't had caffeine, and my night was…well." She drew a deep breath. "But I think she just doesn't know how to deal with the love she feels for you, or even how to show it. Tying you up was symbolic. You get it? You're hers. You're tied to her. You see?"

He was quiet for a moment. "I guess."

"You know what happened before. The two of you

were too hot, too heavy. You didn't share the stuff that scared you. You didn't do the things you need to do to make it last."

"Yeah."

"You burned it out."

"I know." He sounded terrified. "I don't want that to happen again."

"Then do more than the wild sex. Talk. Communicate. Listen to each other. Be there for each other."

"I can do that. But pinning Liza down is hard. She's not exactly the communicative type."

"Well, turnaround is fair play," she said, quoting Jacob.

He paused. "You mean...tie her up?"

"Give the boy an A."

He laughed softly. "Gotcha. Now tell me about your night. You have a bad one?"

Bad? No. Good? No. Try the best night of her entire life. "Hard to explain." Especially since, for Jacob, it had all been..."normal." Heat filled her face at that. *Bastard.*

From its perch still on her floor, the alarm clock went off again, and she sighed. "We've got to get a move on. Get up. Get Liza up. Meet me in the conference room for round two."

"Oh, boy," Eric said. "Here we go again."

Yeah. Here we go.

THOUGH HE COULD HAVE showered and changed at Hush, Jacob went back to his apartment. Right now he wanted to be in his own space. But as he climbed the three flights of stairs, he knew the problem wasn't the outside world, but the thoughts racing inside his own head.

He wished he was still in bed with Em. He wished she was tucked beneath him, while he was buried deep inside her, taking them both to that nameless place of abandon they'd been to several times in the night.

How many women had he been with? Many, and not once when a woman had called out his name while lost in passion had he stopped just to watch her.

With Em, he hadn't been able to tear his eyes away. He loved the way she arched up, her throat open and vulnerable, the way she panted his name in that serrated, husky voice that always sounded so…surprised.

Yeah, that was it. Every time she'd come, she'd been honestly surprised.

Watching her unravel had the been the sexiest, most erotically charged experience of his entire life.

Then morning had come and she had wanted to obsess and tear it all apart and look for the meaning.

And he'd hurt her.

Damn it, he knew he had, but at the time he hadn't cared. He'd been choking, panicking, as he'd stared at her, wanting nothing more than to haul her close, bury his face in her hair, and not let go.

Never let go.

He scrubbed his hands over his face but the longing remained. And he didn't know what to do with it. Why wasn't it gone? Why hadn't one night been enough? One night *had* to be enough.

He came to the landing outside his front door and

stared in surprise at Pru, who was sitting there waiting for him. "I'm going crazy," she said, and rose to her feet.

Jacob unlocked his door, shaking his head when Pru pushed ahead of him and entered.

"Come on in," he said dryly.

"Did you hear me?" She whirled to face him, her neat, long braid nearly blinding him. "I'm losing it here."

"Join the club." He stood in the middle of his living room, glancing toward his shower with longing.

"Jacob."

He sighed. "What's happened?"

"Everything. Nothing."

Jacob squinted at her. "Is that in English?"

"We went out last night, Caya and I. And at the end I kissed her. Caya kissed me back, and I'm telling you, it was real. It was love—"

"Pru—"

"It was," she insisted.

"How do you even know the difference between lust and love?"

She looked startled at the question. "I just do."

"You're going to have to do better than that."

"Okay, well…lust can be sated. Lust is gone when you wake up the next morning. Lust doesn't have those bone-deep terrifying feelings, like you *have* to see that person again or your life is never going to be the same."

Something pinged deep in Jacob's gut. It felt like worry, but that couldn't be it because he never worried. Nothing had ever been worth worrying over. "Sounds like nothing another night of sex wouldn't cure."

"No." Eyes sad, Pru shook her head. "See, you'd think so, but then you get there, and you do it again, and it's only worse."

Shit. *Shit*. She was wrong. She had to be wrong. "Maybe some lust is just more stubborn than others."

"Honey, lust is a fickle bitch, but one thing she isn't is stubborn."

He stared at her, dread clawing its way up his throat. "I see."

Someone knocked at his door. Turning his back on Pru, he opened it and found Caya.

She had wet eyes and a matching misery on her face. Aw, hell. "I suppose you want to join—"

She stuck a finger into his pec, poking hard. "Did you tell Pru she should tell me how she felt about me?"

"Uh—" He glanced back at Pru over his shoulder, but she'd moved out of sight from Caya, flattening herself back against the wall, shaking her head *no,* looking panicked that Caya might see her.

He'd known this was going to come back and bite him on the ass. He turned to Caya, still on his doorstep. "Look, I don't think I should get involved—"

"Well, it's too late now!"

"Caya—" He stopped helplessly when a tear spilled over. "Aw, no. Don't—"

She burst into tears.

"Goddamn it." He pulled her in for a hug, turning her away from seeing into his apartment, though it didn't matter because Pru had vanished into his bathroom. Now that she was out of sight, he moved Caya inside because he figured there was no chance in hell either of them was going away anytime soon.

"See, you do care," Caya sniffed against him.

"Just a little."

She pulled back and looked into his face. "Look at that, admitting it didn't make you choke."

He frowned. "What is that supposed to mean?"

"It means you're just as screwed up as me when it comes to letting people love you, and loving them back." Caya swiped at her wet cheek. "I'm sorry. I know I'm freaking out here, and taking it out on you." She covered her eyes, then dropped her hands to her sides. "Pru said she loved me."

"I know."

"She wants me to tell her how I feel back, but what the hell do I know about this stuff?"

"You're asking me?"

Caya laughed. "Yeah. Fine mess, huh? So do you think it's screwed up that I…sort of love her back?"

"Well, I—" Jacob broke off when the bathroom door behind them opened.

Pru stepped out, hand over her mouth as she stared at Caya.

At the sight of her, Caya jerked as if shot. "Y-you're… here."

Pru nodded, her eyes filling.

"You…heard me," Caya whispered.

"'Sort of'?" Pru whispered.

Caya swallowed. "More than sort of."

Pru's eyes filled. "Oh, my God."

"I didn't want to love you," Caya said. "I tried not to. But you're it for me."

Pru's eyes overflowed, and there was so much hope on her face, it hurt Jacob to look at her. "What about men—"

"They're great, but not what I want."

"Caya, my God. Are you sure?"

"Very. Besides, most men are maturity challenged. Sorry," she said to Jacob. "No offense intended."

"None taken," he said dryly.

Caya turned back to Pru. "I've been out there, I know what's waiting. I don't want any of it, men or other women. Just you."

They reached for each other in an embrace so real, so raw, Jacob had to close his eyes.

When he opened them, they were kissing.

"So." He cleared his throat. "I guess you can both go now."

They kept kissing, passionately. Jacob figured it was a fantasy of men everywhere but for him it only felt like salt on a wound he couldn't see. "You know what? Never mind. I'll go."

They just kept at it, as if they didn't need air, didn't need anyone but themselves.

Jacob grabbed his keys and walked out of his own damn apartment.

12

Note to Housekeeping:
Refill the sensual massage oils and the condoms
in the Haiku Suite.

THE AUDITIONS were worse than the day before, if that
was even possible. *American Idol* rejects had nothing on
the people they saw today, and after several hours, Em
had her head in her hands and Liza had a drink in hers.

"This isn't going to work," Liza said after they'd
seen an eighty-year-old woman from Russia, who could
indeed cook but couldn't speak a word of English.

"No, it's not going to work." A heavy dread was
making itself at home in the pit of Em's belly. "Well,
it's been fun working with you while it lasted."

"You could talk to Jacob."

"No."

"You could beg Jacob."

"Double no."

"Okay, then." Liza put her drink down and picked
up her purse.

"Where are you going?"

"You saved my life. Now I'm going to save yours."

"What do you mean, I saved your life?"

Liza looked at her. "I wasn't asleep when Eric called you this morning."

"You weren't?"

"I was faking it. I've always been good at faking it. I've had to fake it with every man I've ever been with—except Eric."

"Oh, Liza."

"It's because he loves me. I can believe it because he told you. He has no reason to lie to you."

"Honey, he has no reason to lie to you, either."

"I know, but…well, I just couldn't be sure. Love has never been good to me."

Em knew that. Liza's parents hadn't been warm and fuzzy but cold and impossible to please. Liza had been acting up all her life to prove she didn't care. "Eric's the real deal," Em said quietly.

"I'm getting that." Liza's eyes shimmered with emotion. "And that's my point. I can let go, let myself *really* love him, you know? No games, just the real thing. And it was you who helped me see it, that this thing between us can really last for the long haul." She hugged Em tight. "I'll never be able to thank you enough for that. But I'm going to try like hell. You'll see. I'm going to fix this for you."

"You can't—"

"I'm your assistant. It's my job to solve your problems, and I'm going to go solve this. Let's go."

"Where?"

"Just come on." Liza opened the conference door.

Eric stood there with his clipboard monitoring the short line of hopefuls left. There were only two, a girl who looked to be about twelve and an old man who, if she wasn't mistaken, was napping on his feet.

"We need you," Liza said to Eric.

Without question, Eric turned to the two candidates left. "I'm sorry, that's it for today. Thanks for coming."

Liza looked at him as if bowled over.

"So what do you need?" Eric asked her.

Still looking unbearably touched that he'd blindly follow her simply because she said she needed him, she cleared her throat. "Let's go. You'll see when we get there."

As soon as they hit the lobby and walked toward the main entrance of Amuse Bouche, Em hesitated. "He already said no, Liza." Her heart tightened at the memories of last night and this morning. Memories he'd sullied when he'd looked at her as if she'd been any of the other women he'd let in, and then out, of his life.

She hadn't expected that, she could admit, though what she *had* expected, she couldn't exactly say. She'd known who he was, what he was. She'd known his past. She'd known he was wildly, fabulously sexy, with an edge, with a wanderlust spirit, a man who rarely settled in one place for long.

And she'd slept with him anyway, just as she'd also begun to fall for him.

That made her the crazy one, not him.

"Let's just talk to him," Liza said.

"I can't."

Liza frowned. "You look pale."

"Just tired."

"Long night?"

Aware that both Liza and Eric were watching her carefully, she lifted a shoulder.

"I knew it," Liza said. "Oh, honey. Did he break your heart? Because if he did, I can break him. I can—"

"Liza." Em smiled. What else could she do? "Let's just fix one thing at a time."

"Yes. Starting with the show." Liza looked through the empty dining room toward the kitchen, jaw tight, eyes determined. She was a bulldog when it came to this stuff. "Humor me. Give me five minutes."

The restaurant wasn't open yet. No one greeted them so they moved toward the kitchen doors, where they could see lights and hear talking.

Liza knocked.

A pretty brunette poked her head out. Em recognized her as the sommelier from the other night. "Can I help you?" she asked, looking greatly stressed.

"Yes," Liza said. "I heard both of your assistant chefs were out with the flu and that you're in a real bind."

Both Em and Eric looked at Liza in surprise.

The sommelier sighed. "It's true. But I don't know how you heard such a thing—"

"Oh, you'd be surprised what I hear." Liza smiled and offered her business card. "I'm just a guest here, but you can see I'm an assistant producer, so I know how to get things done. Our location director here—" she pointed to Eric "—is an amazing cook. No formal training, but he's doing research for a show. Maybe he could help you out today. You could call our studio for his references."

The sommelier looked Eric over with hopeful curiosity. "Really?"

Eric, as confused as Em, nodded.

"Well…" The sommelier glanced down at the card in her hand, then back up into their faces. "You could come in, meet Chef. He'd have to approve this, of course, which, truthfully, he's not likely to do. He doesn't work with strangers," she said, though her gaze turned bemused when she looked over at Em.

"Oh, we're not strangers to Chef," Liza said with a smile.

Em added her own weak smile. Nope, not strangers.

"Just a sec." The sommelier shut the door.

Em turned to Liza. *"What are you doing?"*

"A favor for a favor. We do something for Chef, and then he'll do something for us."

"Liza, those are not equivalent favors!" Em cried. "One day of Eric's services is not going to make Jacob come across the country—"

The kitchen door opened again, and there stood Jacob himself, looking tall, big, and gorgeously rumpled in his battered jeans and boots and a T-shirt that said Smile, It Confuses People.

"Em," he said in surprise, for one brief beat his face unguarded, allowing her to see the pleasure before it was gone in a blink, carefully masked.

It made her sad to think that what they'd shared last night was going to be just a distant memory.

"Chef," Liza purred. "Eric's an amazing chef. He's offering to help you out today."

"Thank you," he said. "But I don't need—"

"It's a Friday. We both know what this place is going to look like tonight, and that's full to the gills. You can't do it alone."

Jacob looked at Eric. "You cook?"

"Yes."

Jacob turned to Em. "What's the catch?"

Em looked into his eyes and felt her throat tighten. He knew she was here for some reason, and not the goodness of her heart. All his life he'd had to scrap and fight to get by, nothing had ever been handed to him, not friendship, not love, nothing.

She wouldn't do the same thing. *She wouldn't do this Nathan's way.* "No catch."

He crossed his arms, disbelieving.

"I'm sorry," she said. "Coming here was a mistake." And grabbing both Liza and Eric, she turned away.

"Wait."

She went still, then turned back.

Gaze still inscrutable, he'd relaxed marginally, and she knew with a sudden clarity that he'd lied to her. Last night hadn't been the norm for him, it had been just as special, just as amazing, as it had been for her.

And he'd pushed her away because of it. It had been his right to do so, and she understood it all too well.

"Help would be welcome," he said, surprising her.

Eric shoved up his sleeves. "Just tell me where and what."

Em nodded and took a step back to let Eric through. "Okay, then. Good luck tonight—"

"Where are you going?" Jacob asked.

"Out of your hair."

Jacob rubbed his nearly hairless head. "No worries there."

Em stared at him. "What are you saying?"

"I think he already said it," Liza said, looking at Jacob as she rolled up her sleeves. "He needs help. From *all* of us."

EM ENDED UP with a ponytail keeping her hair back and a white jacket over her clothes. But it was the knife in her hands concerning her as she contemplated a stack of vegetables that might as well have been Mt. Everest.

Jacob was moving around, lifting big pots, wielding equipment, working near the hot, open flame, mixing up something that smelled like heaven. Eric was on the other side of the kitchen at the open flame, smiling and joking with Pru, while Liza surreptitiously watched them from her corner, mouth grim.

They'd promised Jacob an hour of prep work. Correction. She and Liza had promised an hour. Eric would stay as long as Jacob was needed, the rest of the night if necessary, because, as he said, the experience would be fun.

From the range, Eric laughed at something Pru said.

Liza pretended not to notice.

Em wasn't as good at pretending. Ignoring what had happened between her and Jacob last night, even for an hour, was beyond her, but she gave it the ol' college try as she reached for a carrot and began slicing. How could he look at her and not remember?

Even as she thought it, Jacob glanced across the room at her, nothing showing on his face.

Was he thinking about what they'd been doing only a few hours before? How he'd touched her, kissed her? How when he'd been buried deep in her body he'd met her gaze and had been unable to tear his away?

Eric laughed again.

Liza set down her knife and walked toward them, a look of intent on her face.

Eric turned to her, smiling until he saw her expression. Then his changed, softened, filled with a look of such hope Em wanted to turn away, but she couldn't.

At the look, Liza suddenly broke into a smile, as if Eric was her everything.

Eric returned it.

Pru moved away, and Eric gently touched Liza's face, kissing her softly before going back to his station.

Liza brought her hand up to her lips, sighed, then went back to her station, as well.

And Em swallowed the inexplicable urge to cry.

"You trying to lose a finger?"

When she nearly jerked out of her skin, two arms reached around her, hands settling over hers. "Easy," Jacob murmured.

Easy? Was he kidding? She could feel his warm, hard chest against her back, his heat, his strength. And she could smell him, some complicated mix of soap and man that was so intoxicating she felt dizzy. "What are we making?"

"Spicy Szechuan noodles with grilled Indonesian tiger prawns for the first course, snapper with tamarind-coconut sauce and bamboo rice for the main course. Then tempura bananas with caramel sauce for dessert."

She didn't even know what half of that was. "Sounds interesting."

"Liar."

Craning her neck, she looked up into his eyes. Despite the tension in his body, his eyes were smiling.

"Do you ever just make burgers?" she asked.

"Yep."

"Burgers tonight would be good," she said. "I could forgo chopping all these veggies."

"Would you rather pick cilantro leaves for garnish?" he asked. "It's easier. Or you could prep spinach leaves for salads."

She'd had no idea how much work went into being a chef, the long hours, mostly on your feet, lifting heavy pots and pans, working near dangerous appliances at high temperatures. "I can handle this."

"I bet you can." His arms were still alongside hers, his hands guiding her fingers into the right position on the knife. "This way, Em, so you'll keep all your fingers, see? Nothing wrong with your way, other than I don't like blood in my kitchen." He spoke casually, showing her exactly how he meant for it all to be done, making it look easy. And having him surround her like that was, well…nirvana. It brought it all back, what it had felt like to be skin-to-skin with him, face-to-face, sharing their bodies, and more. Wanting to see him, to gauge if he was feeling any of the overwhelming emotions she was, she tipped her head up to look at him.

His eyes were on the knife and the carrot but they swiveled to meet hers. "You going to watch what you're doing? Or me?"

"You."

His eyes swirled with heat. "Em."

"The things you said to me this morning." She took a quick peek at the others. No one was paying them the slightest bit of attention. "I don't think you meant them."

"I never say anything I don't mean."

"Jacob." She pushed the carrots away and turned to face him directly. "We made love. We fell asleep together. And it was out of this world. I might not be all that experienced, but I know that much." He didn't say anything, and the first bits of doubt crept in. "Or I thought I knew that much," she muttered.

Beneath his breath, he swore. "You did know that much." She just looked at him, and he swore again. "It was insane how perfect it was," he said tightly. "How's that?"

She felt the smile split her face.

With a groan at the sight, he grabbed the knife and started slicing without her, his hands and fingers moving so quickly and efficiently they were a blur. "It doesn't matter, Em. It's not going anywhere, you know that. You're heading back to L.A., and I'm…"

"You're what?"

"I'm not sure. I'm never sure."

"Because you like to be free to walk when it suits you."

"That's right." He finished the huge stack of carrots and started in on the celery.

"Because contracts, even short-term television contracts for huge amounts of money, don't interest you any more than planning for the future interests you."

He set down the knife. "Thank you for your help."

She'd been dismissed. Well, didn't that suit her. She turned away from him, and suddenly realized they were all alone. "Hey, where did everyone go?"

Equally bewildered, Jacob looked around. "You're stressing out my kitchen."

Em put her hands on her hips. "*I'm* stressing out your kitchen? Are you kidding me? You're the one giving me heart failure—"

"When did I give you heart failure?"

She shook her head and bit her lip so the rest couldn't come out.

He merely hauled her up on her toes and put them nose-to-nose. "Tell me."

"Every time you made me come," she whispered.

Still holding her, he stared at her. Annoyance faded, replaced by emotions that made her swallow hard.

"Is that right?" he asked in that silky voice that last night had driven her over the edge too many times to count.

"Yes."

He set her down. His hands left her. "Flour," he said.

"What?"

He gestured behind her, to what looked like a pantry door. "I need flour."

She narrowed her eyes. Was this yet another test? Or his way of changing the subject?

He just waited.

Fine. She'd get him the damn flour. And then they'd talk. She opened the double doors. Inside were shelves stocked with cans and dry goods.

And Eric and Liza. Eric's hair was wild from Liza's fingers, his shirt gaping, his belt open. He had Liza backed to a shelf, one hand up her shirt, the other down her pants.

As Em's mouth fell open, they jerked apart.

"Sorry," Eric said.

Liza smiled apologetically. "Make-up sex…well, you know."

No, Em didn't know. But suddenly she wished she did.

Jacob shut the door.

"Oh, my," she finally said.

Jacob looked into her hot face, then without a word, took her hand and pulled her back through the kitchen, down an employee hallway and through yet another door.

It was a beautiful room, quite obviously his office, with a black lacquer desk and matching shelving unit, and a large window looking out to the busy city.

A black cat sat on the desk, the cat from the elevator on her first day here. At the sight of them, she gave a soft "meow," rubbed around each of their ankles, and began to purr.

Jacob scooped her up, scratched behind her ears, and then set her down outside the office door.

"Yours?" she asked.

"Eartha Kitty belongs to Piper, the owner of the hotel. Sort of a mascot."

She tried a smile. "You have a nice view here."

"I guess. I look at you and I can't see anything else."

The words stunned her. Thrilled her.

"Em, I want to finish what we started in the kitchen."

"The fight?"

"We were discussing, not fighting. I believe you were telling me how it felt when I made you come—"

More heat flooded her body. "I don't feel like talking about that anymore."

"Really? Why's that?"

"Um…" She broke off when he took a step toward her. She took one back, but came up against the window-sill. She gripped it tight at her sides to steady herself.

He arched a brow.

She returned the gesture. "Because," she said, feeling immature as she crossed her arms.

And aware. Let's not forget extremely aware.

"*Because* isn't a complete sentence, or a reason," he pointed out.

"I don't feel like talking about it," she repeated a little shakily when he slid his body to hers, sandwiching her between the sill and his hard form.

"So what *do* you feel like doing?" His voice was amused, but looking into his eyes, he was anything but.

She bit her lip harder this time. No more blurting anything out! There was no point to it, no point in hashing this out.

"Then maybe we shouldn't talk at all," he decided,

and slid his muscled thigh between hers, bringing it up high, making all her happy spots zing to life. While she was still absorbing that, he slid his hands in her hair, tugged her face close and kissed her.

13

EM PULLED BACK from Jacob's mind-blowing kiss. "Okay, maybe we *should* talk." *Before I let you take me right here on your desk.* She wanted him, so much, but realized that scared or not, edgy or not, Jacob was nothing but heartache waiting to happen.

When he stroked a strand of hair from her face and then left his fingers cupping her cheek she squeezed her eyes shut. "Jacob—"

"I loved watching you."

"Butchering the veggies?"

"When you came."

Her eyes flew open.

He smiled wickedly. "You always seemed surprised, every single time. The sexiest thing I've ever seen, watching you let go."

Just his words **flooded heat** in her veins. "Stop."

"Why are you always so surprised, Em?"

Nope. Talking was a bad idea, too. No more talking, no more kissing. In fact, no more staring at him, either, because he looked so good....

She shut her eyes again.

He stroked his fingers down her throat, then over her collarbone, pushing her sweater out of his way as he went.

Her nipples hardened but she nibbled on her lip and didn't make a sound.

"Haven't you ever come with a man before?"

That got her. Her eyes flew open. She shoved his hand away. "You are so full of yourself."

"Have you?" Undeterred, his hands took each of hers, bringing them around her back, holding them there low on her spine, which brought her entire front up against his.

"Yes, I've come with a man before." His gaze was so deep, so real. How could it be that he could let her in like this, and yet not keep her in? "But not like with you," she admitted. "Never like with you."

"What made it different?" His voice was low, husky. *Sweet.*

Damn it, he was sucking her right back in. "Are you sure you want to hear this?" she asked, and saw the truth. No, he didn't want to hear this. He didn't want to know any of it, but he was as deeply shaken as she. And listening to her was the only chance he had of understanding.

Her own understanding nearly rose up and choked her. God, he was something, all confident and sexy as long as things were on his terms, in his comfort zone.

But as he had with her, she, too, had taken him beyond comfort, and the expression behind his eyes opened her heart and made it bleed. "*You* make it different," she whispered. "There's something about you. About how I feel when I'm with you. There's something between us that I can't resist, even if you can. You take me out of myself, Jacob, whether we're laughing, talking, or making love. And because of that, you make me feel more than I ever have. An orgasm with you suddenly isn't this tiny little ping I have to strive so hard for. It's like…"

"What?" he whispered.

"Like the Fourth of July. A full fireworks display." She looked into his eyes and saw the acknowledgement, that he felt the same. "It involves so much more than just our body parts. For me, it involves my heart."

"Your two friends," he said. "Is it this way for them?"

"I think so."

"Seeing them like that made you hot."

And she wasn't the only one. She could feel him, heavy and hard against her. "They belong together, they have an undeniable connection. It makes me want such a thing for myself."

His eyes grew dark, if that was even possible. "I can give you a connection." Banding his arm around her, he lifted her. He sat her on the sill, then stepped between her legs.

"Jacob—"

"I want you again, Em. I can't think with all this wanting."

It melted her, and in spite of herself, she tilted her face up for his kiss, sighing as he met her more than halfway, leaning in, pressing his body flush to hers.

"I keep remembering last night," she murmured when he took little bites out of her on his way over her throat. "How good it felt…"

"If I say I can't remember, can we do it again?"

She let out a laugh—that backed up in her throat when he tugged her sweater down and exposed her bra, its front hook posing no problem for him. He just crouched in front of her, clicked the bra open, then let out a low breath of desire when her breasts popped free. Carefully, gently, he ran his stubbled cheek over one.

Her nipples puckered into a tight knot, wrenching another sound from Jacob's throat. "You are so beautiful, Em."

"Thank you, but I'm not sure—"

He sucked her nipple hard into his mouth and her thoughts skittered right out of her head.

"We probably shouldn't—" She broke off on a moan when he bunched up her skirt and slid a hand between her legs. "Um…well, maybe."

"Oh, yeah," he murmured roughly, slipping her panties aside to sink a finger into her. Then another. "You're already wet." His thumb spread that wetness around while his fingers stroked her until her vision faded.

"Jacob—"

"I'll buy you a new pair, I promise." Then he tore the flimsy scrap of material away from her and tossed it over his shoulder.

It landed on his desk lamp.

"Jacob—" she choked, but then his fingers were back inside her, his thumb teasing her sensitive nub with little slippery passes while his mouth found her breast again. "Oh," she whispered, unable to form words.

"I know." With his fingers driving her to bliss, she wrapped her arms around his neck and held on for dear life as he took her to orgasm in less than sixty seconds.

"Again," he demanded. He dropped to his knees. With wicked intent, he looked up at her, then stuck his head beneath her skirt. Holding her open with his fingers, he used his tongue to drive her right out of her mind.

Gasping, crying, she fell back against the window, her fingers digging into the wood sill as he took her to heaven and back.

And then again. *"Jacob."*

"One more."

"I can't—" But then he did something fantastically clever with his tongue and lightly clamped his teeth over her, as well, adding his fingers to the mix, and she completely and utterly lost it.

She came back to herself at the sound of the condom packet being ripped open. "My God."

"There's more." He spit out the corner of the packet and rolled the condom down his length. "Hold on to me," he commanded. His skin was hot and damp, the muscles beneath hard and trembling.

"Wait."

His gaze went to hers.

Her breathing was still ragged, but she had to say it.

"This isn't…a normal everyday thing." She opened his shirt, ran her hand down his mouthwatering torso to wrap her fingers around his erection, gliding him against her. "Not for me."

He squeezed his eyes shut, gritting his teeth. "Em—"

"It isn't," she repeated in a shaky voice, and let him inside her, just an inch. "This is different, this is us…" Her body was still pulsing with pleasure, making talking difficult, but she forced it out. "This is *us* making it different."

He let out a ragged groan, his face a mask of pleasured pain, the cords in his neck standing out in bold relief, the muscles in his shoulders and arms as he held her so tense they quivered.

"Say it," she breathed, unable to tear her eyes off him.

"Christ. Yes. Yes, it's different with you." At that, he gripped her hips and thrust powerfully, sinking into her to the hilt, stretching and filling her, an action that ripped a helpless cry from her and a low groan from him.

Putting his forehead to hers, he panted for breath. "Wrap your legs around me. There. *There*." Using the sill as leverage, he thrust into her again and again, leaving her gasping for air, unable to say anything else, which she was certain he did on purpose, but with him filling her, sinking into her with each stroke so fully, so deeply, she didn't care. And with a helpless cry, she came again. He followed her this time, pulsing hard within her, his big body shuddering.

She held on to him through it, clinging, eyes closed, face pressed against his throat, her body absorbing the intimacy, the embrace, the closeness, never wanting it to end.

And he let her cuddle, the most endearing thing he'd ever done, holding her tight to him for a long time, as if maybe he didn't want the interlude to end any more than she did.

"And it's two," she whispered.

"Two?"

"Yeah." She smiled when she felt him kiss her neck. "You owe me *two* pairs of panties."

JACOB GUIDED Em into the private bathroom attached to his office where he soaped her up in his shower, then dried her off before helping her back into her clothes.

And all the while he wondered when she was going to say or do something to ruin the glow.

But she didn't say a word as she walked to his office door.

And in the end, it was he who couldn't keep quiet. "Em."

"I know." Turning to face him, she shot him a brave smile. "Don't worry, I know."

"Know what?"

"That even though what we shared was different for both of us, it's going nowhere."

Right. It wasn't. It couldn't. But just looking at her made his body twitch and his heart ache.

He still couldn't get enough, and more than that, he knew he might never get enough.

With one last smile, so sad it tore right through his heart, she patted his shoulder—comforting him!—and went out the door.

14

EM AND LIZA SAT in the lobby, on a corner couch, going over options. There weren't many. It didn't help that in spite of the shower in Jacob's office she could still smell him on her.

His shampoo, his soap… And it was orgasmically good.

Certainly the sex in his office had been.

She'd never come like that in her life, and she knew enough to be sure that she never would with another man.

He was it.

He was "the one."

After a lifetime of toads, she'd found her prince.

Not that he'd welcome her realization.

"Okay, speak."

Em blinked at Liza. "What?"

"I keep losing you to whatever thoughts are making you alternately grin like an idiot, or look as if your dog just died."

"I'm fine."

"You're in love with him."

"Don't be ridiculous. No one falls in love in just a few days."

"Of course they do. You can fall in love in a day, an hour, a minute."

"You've been with Eric for how long? And you can't figure out if it's love."

Liza smiled. "Oh, it's love. I'm pretty sure it always was. I'm going to tell him tonight. In fact, he wants me to wait for him in his room. I think he's going to pay me back for tying him up. Have you seen the toys in those rooms?" Liza shivered with delight. "I hope we use the fur-lined gloves and a blank tape—"

Em put her hands over her ears. "Not listening—"

Liza pulled Em's hands down. "I'll never forget how you helped me through this," she said fiercely. "I want you to be just as happy as I am."

"What I need is *not* to be picturing you and Eric using one of those blank tapes."

"Well, maybe we won't, maybe we'll just go through the Kama Sutra—"

Luckily Em's cell phone rang, cutting off that thought. It was Nathan.

"You've been seen with the chef," he said without preamble.

"What? How did you—"

"I know all. Now reel him in."

Em grated her teeth. "Nathan, you know I don't work that way."

"Are you or are you not sleeping with him?"

Em's heart clutched. "Whatever I'm doing on my off-hours has nothing to do with work."

"Perfect, you are."

"You're not listening—"

"Just keep at it, Em. This is going to be great." *Click.*

Em stared at her cell phone, dread and regret nearly overwhelming her.

Liza was watching her. "Forget him," she said. "He's an ass."

It helped to remember that but didn't make her feel any better to know that anyone on the outside looking in might assume the same thing as Nathan. That she'd slept with Jacob to convince him to take the job.

What if Jacob thought it?

No. No, he wouldn't. Couldn't. But still, the worry nagged at her. "I'm not going to do this the way Nathan would," she said out loud.

"Of course you're not," Liza said loyally. "You're not going to hurt Jacob. But, honey…is he going to hurt you?"

"No." Her eyes burned. "Maybe."

"Oh, Em—"

"Really. I'm okay." She managed a smile. "I'll see you in the morning. We fly home tomorrow."

"Yes, but—"

"Go. I'm fine." She waited until Liza had left to let her smile fall away. She wandered toward—where else?—Amuse Bouche. Nathan's words still echoed in her ears but she could care less.

She just wanted to see Jacob. It was late, far past the

dinner hour, but the place was still buzzing, filled with groups of people.

No one, she saw, was eating alone.

Well, she'd start a new trend. She was seated at a lovely table, and as she settled in didn't catch a glimpse of the man she'd been with a dizzying amount of times in three short days.

Did that make him her lover?

No, she told herself. A lover implied some sort of relationship, loose as it might be. Lover implied emotions were involved.

Jacob Hill didn't want any of that. Jacob Hill wanted his freedom, he wanted no ties, he wanted—

"Look at you." In the flesh, he suddenly stood by her table in his chef's gear, looking so official, so authoritative, so…outrageously sexy. "Sitting here in my restaurant," he said, "looking like the best thing I've seen all night."

She didn't want to be moved, but damn it, she felt a helpless smile break through.

"Hungry?"

Uh-huh. For you. "A little."

He flashed a grin that was so naughty she felt her nipples go hard. "Well, I do aim to please," he said. "What can I get you? Something sweet? Something hot?"

"We are talking about your food, right?"

He waggled his brows. "Maybe." Then without asking, he pulled out the chair next to her and sat.

"Don't you have stuff to cook?" *Maybe other women to drive insane with longing?*

"We're winding down. It's late." He touched her, running a finger down one cheek. "And you're unhappy."

Turning her head away, she busied herself with the menu. Why had she come? To torture herself? Because if so, she was doing a good job.

"Em."

"You know what?" she said, shutting the menu again. "I'm tired. I should just order room service." She reached for her purse but before she could stand, he snagged her wrist.

Not looking at him, she fiddled with the strap.

"*Em.*"

With a sigh she glanced at him, then was sorry. He was no longer smiling, instead his expression had filled with things that made her want to melt into a pool of longing. "Don't," she whispered, closing her eyes.

"Don't what?"

"Don't look at me like that, like you want to hold me, like I mean something to you, like what has happened between us means something to you, because we both know that none of that is true. When I go home tomorrow, you'll go on as if nothing happened. And me, I'll—" She bit off the words, refusing to expose herself to him again, emotionally or otherwise. "Please. Just let me go."

He looked at her for a long moment, then slowly loosened her fingers. "I'm sorry."

Well, so was she. Sorrier than he could ever know. Letting out a frustrated breath, she stood up. She met his gaze for one long, helpless moment, during which she would have sworn time stood still, would have sworn that he wanted to tell her he felt everything she did.

Because she wanted him as a chef in her show, yes, but she also wanted him as a man. And not just in her bed. She wanted him to be hers. She wanted him to understand that love *could* happen, that it could even happen in a blink of an eye.

Or on an elevator.

It could happen in a year, a month, a few days, it didn't matter. She wanted him to know that when it was real, it was meant to be sought and kept.

Not tossed away.

But most of all she wanted him to understand that what they had, what they could have had, was as real as it gets.

In the end, she didn't say any of that. She just walked away.

And he let her.

THIRTY MINUTES LATER Em was in her room, in the white, fluffy, luxurious robe after a long, scalding shower, waiting for room service to bring the French fries she'd ordered, contemplating how stupid men were.

Because Jacob should be up here. Sighing, she brushed through her newly washed hair. He should be in bed with her right now.

But he hadn't turned out to be much of a mind reader, and she was a grown-up. If she'd wanted him so badly tonight, she should have saved her little goodbye drama until morning.

Someone knocked at the door.

Tightening her robe, she put her eye to the peephole, then her body went as still as her heart went wild, leaping inside her chest, banging against her ribs.

Jacob stood there, still in his chef's uniform.

Em pulled back. *What was he doing?*

"Open up, Em."

Open up. Hadn't she done that? Hadn't she opened up her heart and soul? What more could she give him?

"Em."

She put her hand on the knob, drew a deep breath, then opened the door. "What are you—"

"You called for room service." He gestured to a covered tray at his side, then pushed it past her and into the room.

"But…" She stared at him as he shut the door and lifted the plate covers.

"Crisp pan-seared salmon," he said. "And from Pru I've brought a very nice 2001 Robert Stemmler pinot noir."

She couldn't help it, she laughed.

He raised his face in surprise. "What?"

"I ordered French fries." The ultimate comfort food.

He made a soft sound of disapproval as he looked over the meticulously arranged tray, and she laughed again. "You are such a food snob."

"I am not."

Oh, yes, he was, and he had no idea. Nor did he have any idea how absolutely, stunningly adorable he was. She had a feeling he'd never been considered adorable before.

"Will there be anything else?" he asked.

You on a plate. "No," she whispered, then remembered her little chat with herself. Be honest. Be open. "Yes."

"No or yes?"

"Yes."

"Name it."

She licked her lips and thought about how to tell him that if she couldn't have him in her life, she'd take him for the next few hours. "I want you."

His gaze flicked over her wet hair, her undoubtedly shiny, makeup free face, and then lingered on her robe-covered body.

For a long moment he just looked at her as she grew uncomfortably warm under the terrycloth.

"Well, we do aim to please here at Hush," he said finally, unbuttoning his chef's coat and tossing it to a chair, which left him in his black trousers and a snug white T-shirt that invited the general public to Bite Me in block letters. She smiled.

He wrapped his fingers around the tie of her robe and tugged her to him. "What's so funny?"

"I'd like to bite you."

He arched a brow. "Watch out. I bite back." His hands had easily unknotted her robe. Holding the lapels, he looked into her eyes. "What are you wearing beneath this thing?"

"Um—"

"A sexy thong?"

She shook her head.

"Flannel pj's?"

She gave him a weak smile. Thank God she hadn't put her flannels on. He'd have laughed his ass off. "No," she managed.

"Hmm…"

"Nothing," she whispered. "I'm wearing nothing beneath."

With a groan, he spread the robe open, slipped his hands inside and looked his fill. "You are so beautiful." Sinking to his knees, he put his mouth to her hip, kissing her softly. Then her belly button.

And then lower.

Her hands fisted in his hair. Her head fell back. Then his mouth moved southward—and hit her equator. One lick and she was panting for air, her senses on overload. *"Jacob."*

"Mmm," he said, his mouth full, his tongue… God. His tongue.

"What about the real room service? They might come," she gasped, her eyes rolling back in her head when he did something fantastic and wickedly wicked with his fingers.

"The only one coming is you."

Then he lowered her to the floor, and made good on that promise.

JACOB LAY FLAT on the floor, stripped naked, with an equally naked Em nibbling her way over his body. It was torture, but the best torture he'd ever experienced.

"You've got such an amazing body," she told him, exploring every inch. "Just looking at it makes me want to gobble you up." She licked his nipple, then lifted her head. "I've never said such a thing to a man before."

Oh, yeah. Torture.

"This is my favorite, right here." And she sank her teeth into his inner thigh.

When he jerked, she lifted her head, eyes luminous, breasts swaying. "Do you want me to stop?"

"God, no."

She resumed her activities, taking her mouth on a happy little tour, until she reached his erection and licked it like a lollipop.

He jerked again.

Once more she lifted her head, with an adorable concerned little frown puckering her brow. "Am I doing it wrong?"

Choking out a rough laugh, he slid his hands into her hair and guided her head back. "No."

"Are you sure? Because I can—"

"If you stop again, you're going to kill me."

She let out a slow, sex-kitten smile that had him groaning and his toes curling. He'd created a monster. "Come up here, Em, and let me—"

"No, let me," she murmured in the voice of a pure seductress. "Because this time, Jacob Hill, you're the one coming."

He'd wanted to be inside her when he climaxed, had planned for that with the unopened condom on the floor next to him, but she tore the control from his tightly held reins as no other woman had, with those fingers, with that incredibly soft, sweet mouth, both of which she used on him until his eyes crossed.

He was going to lose it. He was really going to lose it, right here, right now. "Wait," he gasped.

"It's okay."

"No, it's not that—" He couldn't think with the blood running out of his head and his entire body on high alert. "Em— Wait."

But she didn't, and there was something about her slightly fumbling hands and mouth, the endearing inexperience mixed with the sexual yearning that completely and totally undid him.

He exploded. And when he lay there, annihilated, still quivering, humbled to the core and just as shocked, she put her hand on his chest and leaned over him until her face wavered in his view.

"Jacob?"

"Still here. Barely." He smiled.

Hers wobbled. "I love you," she whispered, and destroyed him all over again.

15

Note to Housekeeping:
Guest requested more silk scarves in room 1214.
There's some wild action going on in there!!

"LET ME GET THIS STRAIGHT." Pru blew the steam from her mug of Maddie's coffee and looked at Jacob. "You stood us up last night for that cute little TV producer you accosted a few nights back?"

Jacob had known this was coming. He'd stumbled home from Em's room at dawn. Pru and Caya had dragged him out of bed a short time later, bringing him here for the interrogation. He concentrated on not burning his tongue on his coffee and said nothing, silently pleading the Fifth.

At his lack of comment, Caya raised a brow. "Interesting."

"There's nothing interesting," he said.

"Uh-huh." This from Pru. "You went back for seconds. That's *very* interesting."

"Look, just because you two have found…whatever it is you've found—"

"Love," Caya said, and reached across the table to squeeze Pru's hand.

Pru smiled in a way Jacob had never seen, a soft special curve of the mouth. He sighed. "It doesn't mean everyone has to be just as happy as you guys."

"What's wrong with being happy?" Caya wanted to know.

He stared into his mug and thought about that. Thought about other things, too, things that started with "I" and ended with "love you."

Holy shit, had that really happened? Had he had the most mind-blowing orgasm of his life flat on his back in Em's hotel room floor, and then blinked back to consciousness to find her leaning over him, smiling with her entire heart in her eyes as she said "I love you"? "Nothing's wrong with being happy," he finally answered. "It's just not as easy for some."

"You think it was easy for us to get to the point where we know it's real, that beneath the passion there is enough to sustain us for the long haul?" Pru asked. "Because you know it wasn't easy, not at all."

"I do know. But—"

"No *buts*," Pru said. "Look, Jacob, I think you have this thing, like you believe you somehow don't deserve love and happiness the same as the rest of us." Her eyes were warm as she looked at him. "You're wrong, Jacob. You do."

He frowned at the both of them. "I thought we had an agreement. You two worry about your own lives, and I'll worry about mine."

"By your own words, that agreement was to be null and void once I got my own love life in order," Pru reminded him.

Caya's eyes shone brilliantly at her. "And your love life is most definitely in order."

The affection that shimmered back and forth between the two of them was so powerful it was overwhelming, and Jacob felt his throat tighten. He was really losing it here.

He'd had someone looking at him like that, and he'd walked. What did that make him?

A smart man, he reminded himself.

"Tell us about her," Pru said softly.

"Oh, I'll tell you," Maddie said as she came up to refill their cups. She smiled into Jacob's frowning face, utterly unimpressed by his silent imploring. "She's beautiful, of course. That's what attracted him."

"That is not what attracted me," he said in his defense. "I'm not that shallow."

"You're a man, aren't ya?" Maddie patted him on the head. "She's also sweet and smart, but the most important thing..." She leaned in as if departing a state secret. "She makes him yearn for things he didn't know were missing in his life."

"Maddie—"

She smiled warmly at Jacob's warning, then kissed him sweetly on the cheek. "Oh, luv. Just accept it. She's yours. And you're hers."

Pru and Caya were staring at him in shock as Maddie walked away.

"She *is* different from your other lovers," Pru said thoughtfully.

"Really?" Jacob asked, annoyed. "And how do you know that?"

"Because she lasted more than one night," Caya said.

Ouch. Was he really that quick to move around?

Yeah. He was.

"Tell us more," Pru said.

"Look, there's nothing to tell. She's leaving, so what does it matter?" Was that his voice, sounding shaken at the thought of Em going back to Los Angeles? Maybe he was just tired after the past few nights of incredible, wild sex.

Okay, not just sex. Sex he'd have been able to get past. Whatever the hell they'd done had been more, enough to grab him by the throat and hold on good.

And then there had been those three shocking words he'd never heard directed at him before.

I love you.

"She loves me," he heard himself say.

Pru and Caya stared at him, then burst out laughing.

"What the hell is so funny about that?" he demanded.

"Because every woman falls in love with you," Caya said. "Hell, I'm half in love with you and I'm taken—" She broke off at the look on his face. "Oh. Oh," she breathed, and put her hand to her chest. Her eyes misted. "This one is different," she said softly. "She's different because you feel it back. Oh, Jacob."

"My God," Pru murmured in wonder. "It's happened. And I didn't even have to do a damn thing."

Jacob shoved his fingers through his short hair. "Not helping."

"Oh, honey." Pru grabbed his hand. "Why can't you just admit it?"

"Admit what? That you're a helpless romantic?"

"That you love her back."

"Maybe some of us don't like to wear our hearts on our sleeves," he said. "Maybe some of us have healthy caution inside and don't feel the need to rush into anything."

"Maybe some of us are terrified of feeling it at all," Caya said very softly, and leaning in, hugged him tight. "Is that it?"

"Damn it." He gently pushed her off him and went back to staring into his coffee and brooding.

"You aren't going to be stupid about this, right?" Pru asked. "You're going to go after her, this one-and-only woman who's ever turned your head."

She'd turned him upside down was what she'd done. "I'm not doing anything."

Caya and Pru looked at each other in dismay.

"Look, this little coffee get-together has been sweet, but…" He shoved to his feet and tossed down some money to cover everything.

"Jacob," Pru chided gently. "You can't just ignore it."

Sure he could. Especially when the alternative was something he couldn't even contemplate.

"You can't just walk away," Caya called after him. "You've always gotten away with that, I know, but one of these days it's going to catch up to you."

Maybe. But not this time.

ERIC AND LIZA flew home on an earlier flight than Em.
With a few hours left before she had to leave for the
airport, she sat in the lobby with her clipboard, trying
to put some cohesive notes together for Nathan. Her cell
phone rang. One glance at the caller ID had her wincing.
The boss himself. "How's it going?" she asked him in
the most chipper voice she could muster.

"That's my question for you."

"Oh, everything's fabulous," she said. Which was
sort of the truth. Parts of this trip had been fabulous.

Mostly the parts when she'd had Jacob buried deep
inside her, but that was definitely too much information.

"Have you got him yet?" Nathan wanted to know.

"Actually, I've got several candidates but I've decided to hold auditions in Los Angeles, as well."

"What happened to Hill?"

"He isn't interested."

"I thought you slept with him."

Em closed her eyes and winced. "I am never going
to sleep with someone for my job."

Nathan sighed. "If you're going to be so damn empathetic, at least use it to your advantage. Have it help
you instead of hurt you."

Though he couldn't see her, she lifted her chin. Being
empathetic might have caused her more than a few embarrassing or uncomfortable moments, but it had helped
her. It had helped her become the person she was. If he
couldn't see that, then she couldn't make him. "I'll find
someone just as good. Trust me."

There was a long silence. "You still have three weeks. Work on him."

Her stomach sank. "I'm not going to 'work' on anyone, Nathan." She couldn't. Wouldn't. But sometimes there were other ways, better ways. This was one of those times, she was sure of it. "But if you'd just trust me, I can do this."

"Your way, right?" he asked dryly.

Determination blazed. "That's right."

"I suppose you have ideas."

"You know it." Her mind whirled. "In fact…I wanted to talk to you about a few changes."

"I don't like changes."

"Just listen. I was thinking about a traveling cooking show."

"Traveling?"

"We'd still need a chef, but this person would be almost more like a host, coming to us from a different restaurant across the country each week." Her thoughts raced. "He wouldn't need to be a big celebrity chef. In fact if he's unknown, it'll be better for the ego of the chef at the restaurant we're visiting."

"Hmm."

Not exactly encouraging, but he hadn't said no yet so she went on. "With the spotlight on the variety of settings, people will want to tune in each week to see and learn about a new place," she said earnestly, getting more and more excited. Why hadn't she thought of this before? "No stagnant studio. The restaurant will get promo, the sous or executive chef at that restaurant will get promo, and we'll get—"

"Drama." Nathan's voice became excited. "Love it. Do it. Stay another day and keep thinking. New York is good for you. Oh, and while you're there, find some New York hot spots. You've got a gold ticket here."

She thought of Eric and Liza already cozy on a plane heading west. She was on her own. But that was okay, because she could do this. *She would do this.* She slipped the phone back in her purse and dropped her head, needing air. She'd been given another night here....

"Em?"

Her entire body reacted. Lifting her head, she faced the man she couldn't stop thinking about, even with her career on the line. He wore those battered black Levi's she loved so much because they contoured his body to mouthwatering perfection. Old and clearly beloved, they were soft and faded in all the stress spots, of which there were many. His long-sleeved shirt was black with a caramel-brown stripe that matched his solemn gaze. He stood before her, hands shoved into his pockets, a frown marring that wonderful face.

"What's the matter?" she asked him.

"I was going to ask you that same thing."

"Oh." She forced a smile, trying not to remember that the last thing he'd done with that handsome face had been to bury it in her hair, inhaling her as he squeezed her tight, so tight that she thought maybe he never wanted to let her go.

But he had.

And she had. "Nothing's wrong," she said, adding another smile when he only cocked his head and studied her for a long heartbeat. "Really. In fact, things are great."

He hunkered down before her to take her hands, his gaze holding hers. "Great, huh?"

Oh, God. Physical affection. If she knew nothing else about him, she knew this much—for Jacob it was the same thing as waving a fifty-foot sign saying that he cared about her.

Her pathetic heart rolled over and exposed its underside and she fought an overwhelming desire to throw herself at him. "I'm fine," she repeated weakly.

"But—"

"Jacob. Do you really want me to tell you what's wrong? Really?"

He stared at her, and she could see that running through his head was the moment when she'd blurted out, "I love you," and he'd gone white as a sheet and said, "Thank you."

Thank you.

Yeah, that was what every girl dreamed of hearing from her prince after a lifetime of toads.

"Look," she said, pulling her hands free and standing. "I've got to get to work, which is finally going somewhere."

"You find a chef?"

"I sort of worked around the issue for now."

He nodded, slipping his hands back into his pockets rather than touch her again.

Good, she thought, even as her body missed the

contact with every fiber of its being. She might as well get used to it.

"I thought you were leaving today," he said.

Which would make things easy for you, wouldn't it? "I thought so, too."

"But…?"

Was she wrong? Or had an odd flare of hope flickered in his eyes? "But it turns out I have one more day here."

Nope, definitely a flicker of emotion in those eyes. But the question was, was that flicker just sexual excitement at the thought of having her again? Or more?

"One more night is good," he said very quietly.

And damn if her body didn't quiver. "It's about work," she said. "The show, it's going to be a traveling cooking show. Same host, but instead of an L.A. set, we're going to hit different locales around the states. My boss thought that while I was here, we should be scoping out New York City to stack up a few restaurants."

"Ah."

"So I guess I need to run around to nail down some good places." They both knew he was the man to show her such spots. That Amuse Bouche should be, and was, at the top of her wish list.

Having a show set here, even only once, would be huge. But she had pride, too, and she couldn't, wouldn't, ask him one more time to disrupt the life he appeared to love.

"I have something I should show you," he finally said.

"Really?" She was afraid to read anything into that, into the way he was looking at her.

What did he have to show her? Himself?

"I'm due in the kitchen right now," he said. "But after—"

"Yes?"

"Meet me here?"

He was actually, in his way, asking, not telling. Unable to keep from melting just a little, she simply nodded. She'd meet him tonight.

16

JACOB FINISHED AT the restaurant late and, without taking time for his customary shower and late-night drink with the staff, rushed out into the lobby.

Em stood near the windows, hugging herself, looking out into the night. She wore one of those long flowing flowery skirts he loved on her, and a snug black angora sweater his fingers were already itching to touch. Remove.

As if she felt him coming, she turned slowly, her eyes unerringly meeting his across the filled lobby. And hell if his heart didn't start to pound.

Crazy. He was here only to give her the information he knew would help her search. When he reached her, she licked her lips as if nervous, and he couldn't help it, despite knowing he shouldn't, he leaned in and kissed her.

A little murmur of surprise came from her and for that perfect beat in time, her lips clung to his.

Then she pulled back and smiled at him, more sure of herself now. God, that was something, her sexual confidence. "Ready?"

Her gaze searched his. "I didn't know exactly what you had in mind or how to dress…"

A flicker of unease worked its way through him. "To walk to my apartment? To get the information I have for you?"

Her eyes never left his. "Information."

"When I was getting ready to hire on here, I had a stack of offers. I still have all the files at my apartment. You can flip through them for the spots that interest you. For the show."

"Gotcha." Face carefully blank, she nodded. "Right."

She sounded funny, and that dread grew. "Em—"

"No, it's all good. Thanks," she added with extreme politeness, and turned away, toward the outside doors.

He pulled her back around, having to work at it because she was stiff as a piece of drywall. Searching her face, now so completely shuttered to his, he shook his head. "What did I miss?"

"Nothing." She gave him a smile, a surface-only smile that didn't come close to the warmth and wattage of her real one. "Let's go get the information then."

They walked. The night was chilly, and she refused his sweater, preferring instead to walk at his side, keeping her distance, arms crossed over herself. Through Bryant Park, pretty and peaceful at night, she said nothing. Across the street, toward his apartment building, where they were parted by a pack of teenagers on their way toward trouble, still nothing.

He stopped her at his building.

She looked up at the brick-and-glass front, lit with tiny white lights that no one had bothered yet to take down after the holidays. When he looked at the building, he always felt an odd surge, a sort of marvel that he'd found this place to call his, a nice, easy-on-the-eyes, classy yet warm and welcoming home.

Warm and homey had never been a requirement, and yet now that he had it, it was amazing how much he'd grown to like it. "Home sweet home," he said, and smiled.

She flashed him a quick one, and again it didn't meet her eyes.

More dread. "Third floor."

When he held open the front door for her, she went in ahead of him, careful not to brush any part of her against him, and he found himself leaning in to catch the scent of her. Pathetic.

They walked up the three flights of stairs, and at his door, he tried to turn on his legendary charm. "I can make a late-night snack, maybe a—"

"No, thank you."

He blinked. Had anyone, ever, since he'd begun cooking, turned down his offer of food?

Not once.

"Are you sure?" He nudged her inside. "Because—"

"I'm fine." Still hugging herself, she looked around the apartment without letting a thing show on her usually so vivid face. Not a single inkling of her thoughts.

He looked around, trying to see the place as a stranger would, a glimpse inside his world. And yet all he saw was the huge glass windows, the stark black lines of his leather couch and table, the utter lack of color.

And he saw something else, something more revealing. There was nothing of himself here, no pictures, no personal effects. It wasn't any different in the bedroom, where he had a huge bed, expensive furniture and barely anything else.

Had he thought the place warm and homey?

He showed her the kitchen.

"Oh," she breathed, stepping into the one room in the house he'd made his. Here he had his favorite pots and pans hanging from the ceiling within reach, his utensils in a big copper holder on the counter, his beloved cookbooks out for easy access.

All personal effects.

He felt like sagging in relief at the sight. He *had* put something of himself here. He walked over to a big, fat file near the phone and pulled it out. "This is pretty much a full representation of the best restaurants in the best locations in the city. There are brochures, pictures, reviews..."

She glanced at the file, and then without taking it, looked into his face. "Why did you keep all that?"

He scanned through it. "I don't really know."

"I do. You kept it because you didn't see yourself staying at Hush for longer than it took to get comfortable and settled. You never see yourself staying anywhere, even here."

"I like it here."

"Really?" She moved back into the living area, huge and lush and utterly devoid of...him. "Then where are the pictures of your friends? A fish? Even a plant? Where are the signs that a loving, caring, wildly passionate, beautiful man lives here?"

"You want a sign that I'm here, living and breathing and wildly passionate?" He hauled her up on her toes. "How's this?" And he covered her mouth with his.

THE MINUTE HIS MOUTH touched hers, Em's frustration melted. It had no chance against the onslaught of need and yearning and love she felt for him, none at all. His body was big, burning up with heat, and the easy strength of him such a damn turn-on.

"I need you," he murmured in her ear, then bit down on her lobe, sending waves of erotic desire skittering down her spine. "God, I need you."

A thrill raced through her. Not want, but...*need.* "Really? You *need* me?"

He went still, then pulled back. "I want you," he said carefully.

She shook her head. "You said need."

He stared at her. "I did not."

"It's okay to need me," she whispered, and touched his face. He hadn't shaved that day, and she loved the rough feel of his day-old growth. She ran her fingers over it and sighed. "Because I need you, Jacob."

Still, he just stared at her, stricken. His tough body quivered with tension; whether it was desire, or frustration, or even fear, she had no idea.

Nor did she have any idea how to soothe him, other than wrapping her arms around him.

Not a hardship when his body was like a pagan god's, and so perfectly suited to hers, so able to pleasure her that she was already wet for him as he reached for her sweater. "Want me," she said softly. "Need me. Just take me."

"Em—" he murmured against the tumble of her hair, sounding staggered.

She closed her eyes, absorbing that voice, memorizing it. This was it, their last time. It might have left her hollow but she'd save that for when she was alone again. For right now, feeling him was a relief and a pleasure she wouldn't deny herself. His body felt so good against hers, and that was because it was him. No other man would do. With a slow burn taking root deep in her belly, she put her mouth to his throat.

He made a sound, a rough one, his hands sweeping down her body to her bottom, palming it tightly, rocking her against him.

He was hard, so hard it made her catch her breath. His kiss was demanding, a little rough, as if he was not pleased with how much he wanted this, wanted her.

"Here. I want you here," he demanded gruffly, his hot mouth on her jaw as it worked its way back to her lips, then claimed them in a kiss, a fierce, untempered kiss. Finally his tongue stroked one last time along hers and pulled back. "*Now.*"

"Yes. Here," she gasped when his hands streaked over her already fevered body, beneath her sweater, her skirt, and his fingers slipped in her panties. "*Now.*"

"Take it off, then. Take it all off." Then, before she could, he lent his hands to the cause, doing it for her, stripping her so fast her head spun.

Still fully clothed, he took her hands and held them

out at her sides as he looked her over slowly, thoroughly, his eyes twin balls of heat. "You take my breath away," he said hoarsely.

Feeling incredibly vulnerable, she closed her eyes.

"No," he said. "Look at me."

Somehow she managed to open her eyes again.

"Amazing," he said in a reverent whisper, as if he couldn't believe she was here, for him. Then he slid his hands into her hair and tugged her close again, kissing her long and wet and deep.

She had to touch him. She slid her hand beneath his shirt, and he shuddered, breathing her name. She whispered his, as well, or at least she tried, though it came out more a moan than anything else because his hands were stoking the slow burn within her into flames.

Somehow she got his trousers opened. He was fully erect, hot to the touch, needing release as badly as she, and she wrapped her hands around him.

"God, Em. You slay me."

"Do I? Do I really?" she mused, and stroked him.

They were both lost then. He dropped to his knees and tugged her down with him, tumbling her to the soft rug in front of the fireplace. While he tucked her beneath him, she pulled his shirt open. His body was magnificent, and she had to touch, had to taste, one last time.

Because that thought threatened to intrude, to cool her down, she squeezed it out of her head and licked his nipple, scraped her teeth over it, absorbing the rough sound that came from deep in his throat.

Her insides were trembling, her fingers less than

steady as they skimmed over his chest, over the hard muscles of his pecs, over the tapering line of hair down his middle, and the abs she could never get enough of, all the while finding herself more and more aroused. Because this was Jacob, this was the man who could take her right out of herself. She loved touching him, loved having him touch her, loved how his body was tense and trembling.

She loved him, and bit her lip rather than let it escape again.

He looked into her eyes and knew. "Em," he said in a ragged voice, lacing his fingers through hers, anchoring them by her shoulders. "Don't." He eased her legs farther apart. "Don't hold back because of me."

She looked into his eyes, knowing what she felt was reflected there. Heat and need and so much more it backed the breath up in her throat. Eyes burning, she shook her head. "I won't."

He squeezed his eyes shut, his face tightening in a grimace. "Tell me again."

"I love you."

His eyes opened, deep, dark and suspiciously bright.

"I love you," she said again.

He groaned, then thrust into her, keeping his gaze on hers, letting her see him, see into him, and there was so much there, she let out a small cry and arched up.

He sank into her, again and again, in a connection so heartbreaking and mind shattering, she lost herself. But he found her, held her, and seemed bent on rewarding her in the only way he knew how. Not with words, but with his body. He showed her how high he could take her, how much he could give. It was all too much, she couldn't hold back, and with a fevered cry, she came apart in his arms.

With her name on his lips, he followed her over.

EM LAY ON HER BACK, with Jacob sprawled over her. He was heavy but she loved the feeling of him, hot and trembly, heart still pounding against hers. She hoped he never moved. If they never moved she wouldn't have to face tomorrow.

Finally, with a low hum of pleasure, Jacob turned his head and put his mouth to her throat.

She wrapped her arms tighter around him and held on.

"You okay?" he asked.

"*So* okay."

"We could—"

"No." She tightened her arms on him. "Stay a minute. Right here."

"As long as you like," he murmured.

God, she hoped so, because though the truth burned, she couldn't deny it—she'd stay right here, in New York, in his arms, anywhere…if he'd only ask.

17

IN THE END, JACOB didn't ask anything. Dawn came, and Em finally made herself get dressed and leave his apartment.

Though she'd asked him not to, he walked her back to the hotel to get her suitcase.

Then he caught her a cab for the airport and held the door open for her.

The cabdriver put her suitcase in the trunk and got behind the wheel. Em bent to get in, too, but Jacob wrapped his fingers around her arm and held her back.

"I've got to go," she said, unable to handle a drawn-out goodbye.

He kissed her, and everything else faded away, the sounds of the busy street outside the hotel, the irritated hmph of the cabbie waiting for her, everything except the feel of his fingers sliding into her hair to hold her head, the heat of his body as he pressed his to hers, and the way her heart took one bold leap.

This was not a tentative goodbye kiss, or a maybe-I'll-see-you-around-sometime kiss. It was a hard, emotion-packed I'll-never-see-you-again kiss.

It broke her heart.

Pulling back, breathing unevenly, he stared at her. She stared right back, willing herself not to lose it, not yet. God, not yet.

"Hell," he muttered, and dragging her up on her toes, kissed her again.

Her heart was a big knot in her throat, blocking words, breath, everything but this. She'd lifted a hand to ward him off but it settled on his arm now, digging in, holding on, clinging.

And then it was over. He pulled back, their lips making one last suction sound that pulled at each nerve ending in her entire body.

"Hey, lady, come on," complained the cabdriver.

"Coming," she said, without taking her eyes off Jacob. "Goodbye," she whispered, reaching up to touch his jaw.

He turned his face into her palm, kissed the soft flesh there, then looked into her eyes. And for that beat in time he let her deep inside himself, to a part she hadn't been allowed before. A softer, more gentle side. Quieter. To a place where he had doubts, fears.

But then he blinked and those weaknesses were gone. He again put up his confident, edgy, enigmatic front that nothing could penetrate or disturb.

"Goodbye, Em," he said, and it was as though they had never touched each other, tasted each other. It was as though they were indeed just TV producer and famous chef, two people whose lives had casually crossed.

Never to cross again.

"*Lady,*" griped the cabdriver.

"'Bye," she whispered once more, and to the cab-driver's infinite relief, sank to the seat and shut the door.

She told herself she wouldn't look back, should never look back, but she did. She craned around, and when she couldn't see anything, got up to her knees on the seat and practically pressed her nose to the window, but it was too late. They'd pulled out into traffic, and Hush was gone from view.

And so was Chef Jacob Hill.

THE FLIGHT BACK to Los Angeles was uneventful, at least on the outside.

On the inside, a whole other story.

Hurting, Em sat there in her seat, forehead to the window, watching the country go by.

Somewhere over Arizona, she realized that the old adage that claimed time heals all wounds was full of crap.

Time was making it worse.

With every moment that passed, her heart ached more, her body mourned more. Her brain was having a field day rewinding the memories and playing them over and over and over....

By the time she landed at LAX, her eyes were gritty and grainy, her chest tight with the suppression of tears, and she needed the oblivion of a twelve-hour nap.

While waiting for her luggage, jostled by the other frustrated passengers, she accessed her messages. The first one was from her mom.

"Honey, I know you've been traveling, but you should call your father once in a while. He worries—"

There was a sound like a scuffle, and then her father's voice came on the line. "What she really means is call your mother because she wants to ask you if you've been eating properly, sleeping properly and dating. She wants to know if you're married with kids yet—"

Another scuffle, and a helpless smile came over Em's face as her mother grabbed the phone back. "Honey," her mom said. "Don't pay any attention to him. He's a man. What does he know? Of course you're not married with kids yet. You wouldn't have dared to do such a thing without me. Now remember, call your father."

Em's throat felt thick. Her parents had been married thirty-five years and still acted like kids. Kids in love. How had they managed such a beautiful thing? And why couldn't she come anywhere even in the ballpark?

That thought reminded her of what she'd done these past few days, which was fall foolishly in love with a man who couldn't even think about stepping into the ballpark.

God, she missed him already. She accessed her next message.

"Em, listen to me," came Liza's voice, full of excitement and adrenaline. "The solution has been in front of us all along. We can use *Eric*. Eric as our chef."

Em blinked. Huh?

"He's hot, right? And best yet…he really can cook. I just never thought of it before because, well, I was always too busy being pissed off at him."

Em's brain slowly switched gears from her own misery to her career, where it belonged. Eric. As their chef.

"Think about it," Liza said. "He's been right beneath

our nose the entire time. He says he'll do it if being the host means a pay raise from being location director because he's tired of eating mac and cheese by the end of the month anyway."

A massive exaggeration. Eric, also a true food snob, would never eat mac and cheese. At least not from a box. He'd have it homemade.

"It's a perfect solution," Liza said. "Call us."

Us.

The two of them were an "us" again.

She was happy for them—she really was. More than happy. The two of them deserved everything they found together.

It was just that Em had never been so happy for someone else, and yet so utterly devastated for herself at the same time.

Three weeks later

"WELL, IT'S OFFICIAL." Nathan let himself into Em's office and tossed a stack of papers on her desk, his face utterly inscrutable.

Oh, God. Watching him, her stomach sank to the floor, where it had been a lot since she'd gotten into that cab and left New York and Jacob. She hadn't been sleeping or eating well. She hadn't been doing anything well, much to Liza's consternation.

"You need to get laid," had been Liza's solution.

"I've already tried that," she said.

"I meant with someone new. To forget Jacob."

But there would be no forgetting him.

At the look on her face, Liza had hugged her tight. "Oh, honey. I'm sorry. So damned sorry. I wanted you to have a happy ending, too."

"I'll have my happy ending when this show is a success."

"I meant in the bedroom."

Tell that to the fist around her heart. Ridiculous that one trip and a few days could change her life, but it had.

He had.

God, she missed him, so much.

But this was a new kind of dread now, watching Nathan. It was over. The past three weeks of bone-breaking hard work and traveling and planning and prepping had all been in vain. They'd filmed three out of the six shows the network had asked for, one in San Francisco, one in New Orleans and one right here in Los Angeles, each in a fabulous, exciting, chic restaurant, each with Eric presenting the featured chef.

They'd believed it was working, that Eric had charisma on camera, that the places they'd chosen had been fascinating and interesting, that the concept was a good one that they could continue with indefinitely.

If the network picked them up for a season.

But now, given Nathan's somberness, she had to believe that for whatever reason the network had pulled the plug before they'd even aired. No more filming, no order from the Powers-That-Be for a full season.

Bye-bye career, hello working at Taco Bell. "What's official?" she asked, and then held her breath.

Nathan pointed to the papers.

"Can you be more specific?" she whispered.

He looked at her, and slowly smiled.

Smiled.

"Nathan." It was difficult to hear her own voice over the roar of blood in her veins. "It's possible I'm going to have heart failure right here if you don't use words."

"You're pulling it off." He seemed surprised but inordinately pleased. "The reports I've gotten are all positive. Your early reviews are optimistic. The network is happy. And a happy network, Em, makes a happy happy me."

"So you're not saying we're canceled before we've even begun?"

"Nope."

"And I still have a job?"

"Yep."

"Oh, God." She let out a breath, then a relieved laugh, and then jumped up and threw her arms around him.

Just as she remembered—no hugging the boss.

Backing up with an apologetic smile, she did a little three-sixty dance, then sank back to her chair. "Okay, then. Whew. *Whew.*"

Nathan grinned. "What's the plan for the next few cities?"

"I was thinking Seattle, Miami, Chicago."

"What about New York? I don't understand why you haven't done New York."

Just the words caused a ping low in her belly. "Well, you know, New York seems so obvious."

"Don't be ridiculous, New York has got to be

included. In fact, why don't you use Amuse Bouche, with Jacob Hill? I bet he'd love to have the opportunity to showcase his restaurant."

"I don't think—"

"Are you kidding? What kind of chef wouldn't want the publicity a show like this is going to offer?"

"The kind who could care less about publicity. Trust me." Em shoved her bangs out of her face, her hand shaking. This was not the conversation she wanted to be having. It was better when she didn't think about Jacob at all, which she managed to do for whole minutes. Sometimes. "He's not interested."

"A real shame." He patted her arm and left the office.

Em let out a pent-up breath and sagged into her chair, only to straighten up again when Nathan suddenly stuck his head back in. He had a funny look on his face, one she couldn't quite place as he held out a basket. "This is for you."

Standing up, she took the basket. When she saw the pale pink and black tissue paper, embossed with the word Hush, her heart kicked into gear. "Where did you get this?"

"Just got delivered," Nathan said.

She stared at him, the oddest sensations running through her: confusion, denial and, the worst, hope. "It's for me?"

"That's what it says." He merely winked at her and left.

Em stared down at the basket. If her hands had been shaking before, they were apoplectic now, almost a blur. It had to be from Jacob, but she hadn't heard from him, not once in all these weeks. She'd long ago despaired of ever seeing him again.

Why would he send a basket?

Probably it wasn't from him. Probably it was from the hotel itself, thanking her for all the money she'd spent while there. Yep, that had to be it.

She sat on the corner of her desk and peeled the pretty tissue paper back. At the contents, she let out a choked laugh as her eyes welled.

The makings of s'mores, Chef Jacob Hill style, with house-made marshmallows and the most expensive of chocolates along with fresh graham crackers.

What had he been thinking?

She was running her finger over the wrapped chocolate wondering what it meant, when she saw the note. Setting the basket down on her desk, she pulled out the paper.

Dear Em,
    I'm hoping you're still interested in desserts. I'm hoping you're still interested in a lot of things. Enclosed is my résumé. J

What? What did that mean? Em extracted the second piece of paper, and smoothed it out, her gaze running over the carefully printed page.

She sagged back, laughing as a tear escaped. It was a résumé, formally typed up. Not for the chef's position, but to be "your lover, your friend and bearer of your heart."

He'd gone on to list his qualifications, including being

loyal to a fault, honest to the point of bluntness and willing to make sacrifices to strengthen the relationship.

At the bottom was a footnote that read:

Available for interviews upon request. And by the way, now would be a great time to request an interview.

Heart drumming, she stood up and opened her office door, gasping at the tall figure standing there.

Jacob.

He looked so completely overwhelmingly magnificently gorgeous that he took her breath. And then she looked closer and saw the strain in his beautiful mocha eyes, the tenseness in his jaw, the way he had his hands jammed in the pockets of those beloved battered black Levi's. His hair had grown out a bit, and looked dark and glossy under the harsh lights. She itched to sink her fingers into it. His scent came to her, so familiar her knees nearly buckled.

And as he met her eyes, she felt that fist around her heart loosen very slightly.

"You have a minute?" he asked in that quiet way he had.

Behind him the office staff, mostly women, were all watching with interest. Stacy, Nathan's secretary, was nearly falling off her chair as she tried to get a better look. She was speaking into a phone as though giving a play-by-play, which didn't make any sense, until Liza came skittering down the hall with her cell phone to her ear, stopping on a dime at the sight of them.

"Em," Liza said, shoving her cell phone in her pocket after a glance back at Stacy, who hung up her phone, looking guilty. "I need to talk to you."

Em gestured to Jacob. "I'm kind of in the middle of something—"

"I know." Liza came close and looked at Jacob. In a very low voice she said, *"Why are you here?"*

"Liza," Em said, horrified at the unfriendly tone.

"No, I want to know," Liza said in quiet fury to Em. "Because for three weeks you haven't been yourself, you've been sad and grieving and not eating and not sleeping, and just today I thought you were getting better, that you were getting over him, but now here he is, ready to sleep with you and then walk away again. I'm not going to have it, Em. You're strong, so very strong, and I love you too much to let an egotistical jerk-off—"

"Excuse me," Jacob said. "I'm right here."

Liza barely spared him a glance. "I mean it, Em. He's only here for the sex—"

"Until three weeks ago," Em reminded her, "sex was all you were interested in yourself. So, Ms. Pot, please. I think I can handle Mr. Kettle."

Liza looked at Em for a long moment, and nodded. Then she subjected Jacob to a long, withering stare.

Em thought he would offer Liza some pithy remark. She didn't expect him to speak with quiet earnestness.

"This is the second time I've said this," he said to Liza. "The first time was to Eric, and it turns out I was wrong. I'm not wrong this time. I'm not going to hurt her. Not ever again. I promise."

Liza stared at him for a minute more, then gave another nod and turned to leave them alone.

"Can we talk now?" Jacob asked.

The rest of the staff were pretending to work but hanging on every word.

"For someone bearing chocolate," she managed to say in a normal voice. "I can definitely talk." She brought him into her office and shut the door on their audience.

Em tried to keep it together as she lifted Jacob's résumé, silently asking him to tell her what it meant, even though she thought maybe she knew. God, she hoped she knew. "Impressive," she said.

"I was thinking we could discuss terms." He nodded to the résumé. "I still don't want to be on your show," he said very gently.

"I didn't think so." A lump blocked her throat at the worry in his eyes. "It's okay."

"You look great, Em."

She had black circles beneath her eyes, she'd forgotten to put mascara on that morning, and her hair...she couldn't bear thinking about her hair. She was wearing her last pair of panties because she hadn't had the energy to do laundry, and she thought that if he said one more nice word, she would do the unthinkable and burst into tears.

"I've missed you," he said quietly.

Oh, damn. She blinked hard.

"I was a fool." He took a step toward her. "A complete fool to let you go. A cowardly one, too." Another step, and then another. "All my life I've walked away from commitment, from relationships, from anything that was more than skin-deep." One last step put them face-to-face, only inches apart. "But when I was with you, Em, I realized something."

She could scarcely breathe. "What's that?"

"I don't want to be that guy anymore."

It was painful, so painful, to look at him because she knew she couldn't keep the hope out of her voice. "What are you saying?" she whispered.

"I'm saying there's a lot more between us than passion, though that's pretty damn great. I'm saying I love you back, damn it."

Oh, God. "Jacob—"

He put his hands on her arms. "And I know you're here and I'm there, but I'll take the executive chef position if I have to and only work once a week at Hush. Or I'll start over somewhere else, somewhere here—"

She put her fingers over his mouth, and then because words failed, she just looked at him for a minute. "That you'd even do that for me... The show is a success, Jacob. It doesn't need me every day anymore. I'll have to come up with a new show now to produce, of course, but I can do that anywhere."

He wrapped his fingers around her wrist and gently pulled her hand from his mouth. "Keep talking."

"I loved New York. Enough to maybe give the city a shot. I'm sure there's something I can do there, because I know how much you want to be at Hush. That is…if you'd like."

"I don't care where we are, as long as we're there to-gether." His eyes glittered. "So, yeah. I'd like."

"So." She held up his résumé. "The job of holding my heart. You seem uniquely qualified for that."

Slowly his tension seemed to drain. And for the first time since he'd stepped inside her office, he let out a slow smile, one infused with obvious relief. "You think so?"

Nodding, she smiled. "And I am hiring you on the spot for all the above, to be my lover, my friend and the bearer of my heart. As long as I get to be the bearer of yours."

"Always," he whispered fiercely, his arms banding tightly around her as he lifted her up. "Always."

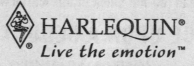

HARLEQUIN®

Blaze™

COMING NEXT MONTH

#237 ONCE UPON A SEDUCTION Jamie Sobrato
It's All About Attitude

He's *so* not Prince Charming. Otherwise Nico Valetti wouldn't be causing all these problems for Skye Ellison. Not the least of which is the fact that she can't keep her hands off him. And since she is traveling in a car with him for days on end, seducing him will just be a matter of time.

#238 BASIC TRAINING Julie Miller

Marine Corps captain Travis McCormick can't believe it when Tess Bartlett—his best friend and new physiotherapist—asks for basic training in sex. Now that he's back in his hometown to recover from injuries, all he wants is a little R & R. Only, Tess has been working on a battle plan for years, and it's time to put it to work. She'll heal him…if he'll make *her* feel all better!

#239 WHEN SHE WAS BAD… Cara Summers
24 Hours: Island Fling, Bk. 3

P.I. Pepper Rossi had no intention of indulging in an island fling. She's at the romantic island resort simply to track down a priceless stolen painting. Only, with sexy ex-CIA agent Cole Buchanan dogging her every step, all she can think about is getting him off her trail…and into her bed!

#240 UP ALL NIGHT Joanne Rock
The Wrong Bed

Devon Baines can't resist the not-so-innocent e-mail invitation. And once he spies Jenny Moore wearing just a little bit of lace, he doesn't care that he wasn't the intended recipient. Sparks fly when these two insomniacs keep company after midnight!

#241 NO REGRETS Cindi Myers

A near-death experience has given her a new appreciation of life. As a result, Lexie Foster compiles a list of things not to be put off any longer. The first thing on her list? An affair with her brand-new boss, Nick Delaney. And convincing him will be half the fun.

#242 CAUGHT Kristin Hardy
The White Star, Bk. 3

With no "out" and no means to reach the outside world, Julia Covington and Alex Spencer are well and truly caught! Trapped in a New York City antiquities museum by a rogue thief isn't the way either one anticipated spending the weekend, but now that it's happened… What will become of the stolen White Star, the charmed amulet Julia is meant to be researching? And what *won't* they do to amuse one another as the hours tick by?

www.eHarlequin.com

HBCNM0206